Answer Me, Answer Me

Also by Irene Bennett Brown

Answer Me, Answer Me

Irene Bennett Brown

WISE WOLF
BOOKS

WISE WOLF BOOKS
An Imprint of Wolfpack Publishing
wisewolfbooks.com
701 S. Howard Avenue 106-324
Tampa, FL 33609

Cover design by Wise Wolf Books

Paperback ISBN 978-1-957548-43-2
eBook ISBN 978-1-957548-42-5

To COREY, LUPE, and CASSIE BROWN
A book for you with love.

Answer Me, Answer Me

Chapter One

I waited for a Greyhound bus to take me the last hundred or so miles to Greendale, Kansas, comparing myself to Dorothy who was set down by a tornado in the alien land of Oz. For me, too, so many things were weird, different, new.

Like packing last night to leave my place in Salem, Oregon; then the chilly rain had made it seem more like winter than early summer. Here outside the Kansas City depot this evening, the diesel-heavy heat was stifling. Still, I preferred it out here to being inside, where sleazy characters hung around making me feel more nervous than I already was.

Flying for the first time was scary, but exciting—one day, and here I am. It hadn't seemed as if we were traveling so fast; it had been more like sitting in a nice chair at the dentist's, reading magazines. Whatever, I'd come too far— it was too late—to rethink what I was doing.

Anyway, by nature I'm a finisher, I have to see things through till they're done. A good thing, because even after I boarded the plane at ten, this morning, it seemed that Gram might reach from the grave to stop me.

In the suitcase at my feet were enough new clothes for two weeks. With good luck, that would be enough time to follow the lead of the clipping and find out who I really am.

It was hard to guess what I might learn. For sure, the clipping and my newly found birth card weren't much to go on. But they were more than I'd had before in my eighteen years. I had to find out more than my name, Bryn Kinney, about all that Gram would ever tell.

For a moment I watched my image in the depot window without really seeing, instead hearing Gram's tight-lipped voice telling me: "You don't have a mother and father, they don't exist. That's all there is to it."

I hated risking Gram's temper when I was little, so I didn't ask questions often. No amount of begging to know about possible relatives somewhere had ever done any good, anyway. Gram was one block I could never get over or around.

As I grew up, I occasionally went through periods when I was so occupied with the present, the moment at hand, I didn't think or mind about not knowing my past. At holiday times, though, I'd be reminded. I would see other families gather to celebrate, driveways filled with cars, picture windows with families gathered at the table. Or other schoolkids would make trips to visit relatives. I wanted to be *them,* then. Gram and I seemed unnaturally alone.

As I got older, I began to suspect that my mother and father might be alive somewhere but didn't "exist" for Gram. I'd think maybe my parents were criminals, murderers serving time in prison—something so bad that it had sealed Gram's lips for good, providing she was my real grandmother. I had my doubts. For all I knew, the taciturn old woman I called Grandmother could have kidnapped me from my real family; she might not have been my blood relation at all.

I had a lot of questions, but no answers.

At the moment I wished the bus would hurry and come. It was starting to get dark; the streetlights had popped on. I fanned myself with the romance novel I'd been reading on the plane, aware that the man in a tacky brown suit a few feet away was staring at me. I gave myself a going-over in my mind: a medium-tall girl with a small bust and waist, long-legged in willow green slacks, and a loose white shirt. Thick brown hair newly bobbed at shoulder length; gray-green eyes, small nose. Full lips and, just below them, a dimpled chin. Overall a bit rumpled, maybe, and needing fresh lipstick, but pretty much all-together on the outside. The inside was a different story. Inside i was as scared and unsure of myself as a little kid.

"You all right?" the man in brown muttered suddenly. "This awaitin' for a bus gets tiresome, don't it?"

Something must have shown on my face, the fear or worry I was feeling, for him to ask. "I'm fine," I told him.

"Beg pardon?"

"I'm fine," I spoke louder. That was one of the problems I meant to work on; I had a soft voice and people often asked me to repeat. I would learn to speak up.

My thoughts went back to Gram, and I slumped down to sit on my suitcase, still fanning. Gram wasn't a talker. But she could have told me a few things about my beginnings, harmless bits of history, like where we were from, who our ancestors were and what they did; what sort of people they were. I wished so much to know all those things. But from Gram, *nothing*.

That's one of the things that still bothered me, remembering Gram. All those chances to talk, to get to know one another's views and feelings, passed by. Opportunities to know one another dried to dust, like seeds without a chance to germinate. But not because I wanted it that way.

I squirmed a bit on the suitcase. I didn't enjoy thinking bad of a dead person who couldn't defend herself, yet in a way I hated Gram, and I wondered if she had really cared for me. There certainly had been no warmth between us: little laughing and talking together, or touching. Gram wouldn't have it, and I tried enough to know. If she wasn't my real grandmother, that might partly explain it.

I remembered that mixed-up day, April second, when Gram died. It was unseasonably warm, a sweet day early in the spring. I was restless in school all day, wanting to be outside where hyacinths and daffodils were in full bloom. I planned to take a long hike after dinner, have nice daydreams about wonderful things I might do someday. Only, the minute I got home from school and stepped into the house, I knew something terrible had happened.

Potatoes burning on the kitchen stove made an awful stink, and there was smoke. Gram was on the floor by the kitchen table, cold when I touched her and she wouldn't move. Things got blurry. I ran from the house screaming, I was so scared. Neighbors we hardly knew came to help out, made me sit down and drink something that burned and made me choke. Somebody called the proper authorities, and in a while, a medical examiner came. "Your grandmother is gone," he said quietly. "She died of natural causes. Nothing could have changed it; she didn't suffer."

I still found it hard to believe.

"Now somethin's wrong, Miss, I know it." The man in the brown suit interrupted my thought. He shuffled up to me and reached out a hand, but I pulled back.

I got up from the suitcase, wiping away tears I'd hardly been aware of. "There's nothing wrong, really." I tried to smile and look comfortable so he would leave me alone. None of the others starting to come outside for the bus were paying me any attention, why should he? I got a tissue from my purse and blew my nose.

I knew too well that guilt as well as grief was behind my tears. Because of the feeling I had after Gram died— the feeling that I was finally free. I was ashamed of that, but how could I help such feelings? When Gram was alive we had stayed to ourselves so much, a cold, lonely, shut-off life. Together, but anything but close.

In that first freedom, I had to learn to do a lot of things. Not just the funeral and settling up—those I had help with, but paying rent after Gram was gone, buying groceries, taking care of all the everyday worries a person has to see to when they live alone. To tell the truth, I liked the challenge. I felt up, I felt capable. I asked for a full-time job at J.C. Penney's, instead of part-time clerking as I'd been doing through most of high school to pay my way. They gave it to me, the day after I graduated.

It was about then that the aloneness set in. I realized what a big part of my existence Gram had been, all those years we'd lived in the old Lost Creek store building, and later, when we'd moved to Salem after Gram's health began to slip. Despite scrimping and scraping and going without, in spite of her cold, unfriendly nature, Gram arid I had shared life. Watching our small black and white TV; she read her tattered westerns at one end of the couch while I studied at the other. Eating meals across from one another. There had been some good to it. The presence of another human being, simple company, had its value. Now, I didn't even have Gram, real grandmother or not.

I shifted a few feet from my suitcase, starting to pace, loosening the collar of my shirt. It was going to be late when I reached Greendale. After ten, probably. I hoped I wouldn't have trouble finding a place to stay. So many things were new, due to my lack of experience. I'd manage, though. I wanted to become a capable, independent person, with a really neat career someday. It was part of my plan for a new me. Making arrangements to come here to Kansas was the biggest step I'd taken so far. Frankly, I was proud to have accomplished it. So far, so good. But I couldn't have done a lick without *the money*.

Soon after Gram died, a banker from the First Community Bank called me to come in and see him. He told me of the savings account Gram had held in trust for me, a fund of nearly eighty thousand dollars. Naturally, I didn't believe him. I didn't call him crazy, though I thought it. It had to be a joke, a hoax, or maybe a give-away TV show, I decided. I knew there was no way Gram could have put money away for me. We had barely made ends meet, from my earnings clerking part-time at Penney's, and Gram's skimpy pay from odd jobs cooking, cleaning, and sewing for other people. There had never been enough then for the extras I would have loved, like magazines, nail polish, perfume. There was barely enough for necessities. Just forget a fortune like that.

The banker kept saying it was true. And the money was mine to do with as I pleased since I was eighteen, and Gram, my legal guardian, was dead. I was shocked, to say the least. Somehow I had the sense to ask for more information, but the banker couldn't tell me much. Just that for about fifteen years an unnamed party had evidently sent Gram a check for two-hundred seventy-five dollars each month. She cashed the checks elsewhere, then banked the money with him. It was not his business to inquire about her methods if she didn't want to tell him. Like most people, he thought her an odd, quirky old woman not to be argued with as long as she wasn't doing anything unlawful, and he couldn't see that she was.

She was keeping a secret, of course. I was sure the money had a connection with my vacant past. No money had come after my eighteenth birthday the end of March. It didn't take a genius to tell me that the money was some kind of support money until I was of age. From a father or mother I'd never known, I guessed.

The hardest part to figure out was why Gram hadn't spent some of the money when it could have made all the difference in the way we lived. As far as I could tell, she hadn't used a dime of it. Maybe the money was tainted, to Gram's way of thinking. The banker felt Gram kept it aside, gathering interest all that time, for me, in case something happened to her. I don't know. It was a strange thing to do, and I still hoped to find out more about it.

" 'Comes the bus," the stranger in brown announced. I thanked him, but I don't think he heard me. Everyone began to move, picking up their things. I tucked my book in a side pocket of my tote with *Vogue* magazine, slung the strap of my purse over my shoulder with my camera bag, then took the tote in one hand and my suitcase in the other.

There wasn't much light to see by on the bus, and I

caught only glimpses of some of the other passengers as I found a seat. A crone of an old woman sat across the aisle from me; a black couple sat a few seats back from the old woman; a hippie-looking guy with a faceful of hair was on my side up ahead. Mainly I was aware that they were strangers, all of them, and I was alone and a long way from familiar Oregon. I bit my lip, trying to stop a nervous cough.

A dark-skinned guy in his early twenties took the seat in front of the old woman; he looked directly back at me, then looked again, more slowly. I drew a sharp breath, not liking the way he grinned at me, kind of surly, on the darkened bus. He wore a black patch over one eye. I curled sideways, knees up on the seat so there wouldn't be room for anyone to sit beside me, positive this bus had taken on the scrungiest, most threatening bunch in the world.

I drew a few deep breaths, hoping it was my imagination that had me feeling so edgy and scared. The bus driver got on and I was thankful that he, at least, looked normal. I could breathe easier for a while after we pulled away from the station. Then the boy up ahead, the one with the eye patch, began looking at me again. I reached up and flicked off the little light above my seat, glad for the cloak of darkness. Though just when I turned it off, I noticed something I'd missed before: he was pretty cute, darkly handsome. But then, I knew the dangerous ones often are.

For all I knew, the guy was planning to mug me or something the moment I got off the bus. I should have arranged my arrival for the morning, it would have been better, safer, in daylight. Live and learn.

We must have been moving for close to an hour when it dawned on me that the guy might have been staring because he thought I was pretty. I hardly ever thought of myself that way so it was hard to remember that someone else might. I didn't always remember that I looked pretty good these days.

I rested my head against the seat, remembering that for a while after I realized the money was truly mine, I still didn't spend any of it, but went on as always. Then, one day at about the end of April, I saw a blouse in a vintage clothing shop in Salem, a gorgeous shirtwaist of eyelet-embroidered white lawn, trimmed with narrow tucks and lace inserts. I wanted it more than any blouse I'd ever wanted before, but I was two blocks away from the store before I realized the blouse could be mine. The next day, I drew money from the account to pay for it; *and* a 1920s-style beaded bag, *and* a mother-of-pearl and silver ring I found in the same shop.

It was easy! And that day marked the start of the Bryn Anne Kinney makeover. I got busy. I had my heavy hair cut in a trim, fashionable pageboy style I picked from a copy of *Vogue,* or maybe it was *Bazaar.* (I'd taken to studying them religiously for things I could do to fix myself up.) I let a cosmetologist teach me how to apply makeup, and I blew a small fortune on lotions, lipsticks, blush, eyeshadows and such. The improvement in my looks (a miracle!) encouraged me, and from then till now I'd lost fourteen blimpy pounds. I bought a svelte new wardrobe: underwear, nighties, shoes, dresses, designer jeans, the works. After years of going without, I nearly went crazy. I was a whirlwind, spending money every spare moment most of May.

I found a small car, a Honda only four years old. Gram hadn't owned a car when she was living. I was thankful I had the brains to take driver's ed in school. I had a license to drive in no time. Then I found a nice furnished apartment to move into near Pringle Park. But I never made the move. I was packing when I opened Gram's old black suitcase that she kept her spare dresses in. I thought I'd give the suitcase and the clothes to Goodwill. The suitcase slipped from my hand, and as it fell it banged on the edge of a chair. A piece of yellowed paper, which must have been caught under a bit of torn satin lining for years and years, jolted loose and fell out.

The clipping was tucked in my wallet this minute, but I didn't need it out to remember exactly what it said: *Greendale, Kansas. October 6, 1925, Ivana Jones left today on another sojourn with the Kinney Movie Company. Ivana is an accomplished organist whose skills add much to the moving pictures.*

My first thought reading the clipping was that it was about someone I didn't know. In all my eighteen years I'd never seen Gram touch a musical instrument nor had I even heard her sing. But Ivana was Gram's first name. And Kinney, the name of the movie company, was our last name. It had to be about her, somehow. At the same time, it was next to impossible to picture Gram playing the organ, and my mind was mostly on that when it struck me that in my hand was the *name of a place where Gram had once lived, Greendale, Kansas*.

Small clue though it was, I remember shaking like a leaf, holding the piece of paper in my two hands as if it were diamonds. Because Greendale, Kansas, was also listed on my birth registration card! Until Gram's death, I'd never seen the card because it was always Gram who took care of things like registering me for school, obtaining my social security card, and so on. At the time I found the card, I thought she'd probably made up the name, Greendale, Kansas, for my birthplace. It sounded made up. But now I had the newspaper clipping, too. I had a match!

I tore through things like a bear after sweets, but there was nothing else in Gram's belongings that mentioned an earlier time, or a place where we might have lived. No letters from relatives, nothing. She'd done a great job keeping nothing that might have to do with our past life; there was nothing to do with me before the age of three. I tried calling the Kansas State Health Department only to be told that my original birth records were sealed, and as far as they were concerned those records were nonexistent.

On the spot, I decided to go to Kansas and do my own digging. Working backward, I'd start with Gram and Greendale where she lived—up to possible information about myself. I'd talk to people; look into other kinds of records that'd be open. Whatever I needed to do for the answers.

Outside the bus window, the lights of a small town were sliding by. I saw them through a film of tears as I felt again the thankfulness at finding the second small clue that might unlock my identity. That might, if I was lucky, lead me to family, to relatives I'd never known. Or into danger of some kind, but no way did I care to dwell on that.

Chapter Two

It was close to another hour before the bus ground to a halt in front of a country diner and the driver announced a forty-five-minute rest stop. I got to my feet, stretching to ease the tiredness and tension in my body, and I filed out of the bus with the others. I wasn't hungry, but the lighted windows of the diner looked homey, welcoming.

A waitress with a handful of menus pointed to a long table in the center. "You passengers who came in on the bus sit over here together so we can take care of you all at once. Over here, please."

I took a chair. The guy with the eye patch took the one next to me, his sturdy shoulders brushing me as he sat down. I studied him as secretly as I could, and I found he didn't look half so mean and threatening here in the well-lighted diner. In fact, he didn't look bad at all, he was *very* good-looking I saw now.

When we got off the bus, I'd seen him run a comb through his thick wavy hair and adjust the eye patch. Now I could see that his one good eye was deep blue under unusually heavy, tangled brows. (I could have fixed them with a few strokes, a thought that nearly sent me under the table.) Instead, I continued to look, unable to help myself. His jaw was square, his lips full. At the open throat of his pale blue striped shirt, his skin glowed a nut-brown. I sat up straighter, forcing my eyes away. Still, I felt stupid, remembering my earlier impression; he was a totally different guy from the one I'd summed up on the bus! I looked back at him, wondering at my blindness.

He caught me staring, then, and he smiled, just as the waitress came. He ordered a double cheeseburger, fries, and a chocolate shake. I ordered iced tea, hoping it would revive me, and a grilled cheese sandwich, although I didn't really want one. Soon, the other passengers up and down the table were chatting comfortably with each other. I relaxed listening in, but I felt sillier than ever.

The soft-spoken black couple were on their way home from St. Louis after visiting their grandchildren. They looked gentle and kind here where I could see them, like anybody's grandma and grandpa. The hairy-faced man I had tagged as a hippie revealed in shy, perfect English that he was seeing America before returning to Oxford University in the fall. And the little gray-haired crone nodding so tiredly over her coffee didn't look to have the strength to squash a flea, let alone hurt me. I felt ridiculous, and glad these people didn't know what I'd thought of them earlier.

I knew I should stop being scared and suspicious of every little thing. If I was ever to grow up and be the way I wanted, I needed to learn to strike a happy medium between trust and gullibility. I kept my face lowered to hide the heat in my face. Then the guy with the patch spoke to me suddenly in a mild, midwestern twang, "Where are you headed, stranger?"

I cleared my throat, "Uh, me? G-Greendale—"

"No kidding? Me, too." His thick eyebrows arched in an expression of delight, and his uncovered eye seemed to twinkle. "I live there. But it beats me why a sleek city girl like you would want to go there."

A piece of sandwich caught in my throat. Sleek city girl? How far wrong could a person get? Thank *Vogue* for my new look; it was working. "My—grandmother died recently and—I had a little time for a vacation." I noticed him lean forward to hear better, so i said more clearly, "I was curious about where she used to live, in Greendale. I came to explore. For fun," I thought to add. No need to tell him my real reason for being here right off.

He asked, "And you came from where?" But before I could answer he held up his hand and grinned. "No, let me guess. Somewhere out west. You sound western, West Coast. San Francisco? LA? Seattle! Right? I go to school with kids from out there."

"Salem, Oregon," I answered in surprise. "You're close." Then I knew that even though he looked all right now, I was telling him more than was necessary. I turned my attention to my tea, faking an interest in the ice beads covering the outside of the glass, rubbing some of them into oblivion. But maybe he could tell me something about where I was going. i took a breath and plunged, "Can you tell me about Greendale? I don't know much about the place. I've never been there before."

"Do you want the catalog tour or my opinion?" He grinned.

"Either. Both."

"AH right." He leaned an elbow on the table, his head in his hand, as he got ready to explain. "To begin with, most people would say that Greendale is way out in the middle of nowhere, a fair enough description. To be specific, the town is deep in the Chase County Flint Hills. Nice country, noted for its bluestem pastures, where cattle get fat and ranchers get rich. Matter of fact, Greendale used to be a rip-roaring, wide-open cowtown where just about every day—according to legend—some hothead cowboy with pearl-handled six-guns . . ." He spoke with a low, exaggerated voice. ". . . shot up the town."

"How about now?" i coughed, fingering my bracelets, wishing talking was as easy for me as it seemed to be for him.

"Oh, now it's peaceful, quiet." He nodded. "I guess you'd say that Greendale is modern and old-fashioned at the same time. A pretty town. At least I think so. Most of the streets are shaded by elm and maple trees. We have a couple motels, and downtown, a hotel. Three restaurants; grocery stores; a bank, schools—the usual. In the city square, they have a bandstand where they still hold concerts on summer nights, just like in the old days. East of town there's a lake where people water-ski and swim. There's a park out there."

"Sounds nice." The truth was, I liked it already from his description.

"What'd you say?"

"It sounds nice, really nice."

"Oh, it is. And it'll be nicer with you there."

I felt myself blushing. He was flirting, but I couldn't think of anything to say back to him.

"Do you have a place to stay?" he asked me then.

I shook my head. "I've been a little worried about that."

"Don't worry. Greendale has a hotel, but it's pretty spendy. If I were you, I'd take a room at Thistle Down

House. It's a big, old English-Tudor-style house right downtown. Used to be a private home, but now they take in boarders. It's not fancy, but it's clean and inexpensive. The Gannaways own it; good people, Louise and Matthew Gannaway. When we get into town, I'll take you there if you want."

I hesitated, then nodded. "All right." I couldn't see any harm, and I hadn't been sure how I'd go about finding a place to stay when I got to Greendale, especially late at night. I'd been thinking about a hotel, but they were expensive. If I wanted any money left for my future, it was time I started to watch my finances more carefully. I added, relieved that he'd made the suggestion, "I appreciate your help."

"Of course, I ought to know who I'm helping." He held out his brown hand, and his long fingers snugged about mine. "My name's Romney Elliot. Rom for short, or Elliot."

"Bryn Kinney." The moment I said my name, I regretted spewing it out like that, but his touch had thrown me off. I should have remained anonymous until I knew more about Gram's life here. It was possible something dreadful happened in Greendale, terrible enough to make Gram keep the place a secret to her dying day. But it was too late. Romney Elliot, at least, knew my true name. It was too late to make one up or take it back. If my last name sounded familiar to him, though, he didn't show it. "What about you?" I asked. "Are your parents ranchers? What do you do in Greendale?" Maybe if I kept him talking about himself he wouldn't ask me any more questions.

He chewed a moment before answering. "Mom and Dad have a little farm, but they're not your typical farm folk. As long as I can remember Dad has been a county

agricultural extension agent. Advises farmers about farming. Right now the folks are leading a farm study tour
over in Europe, chasing about all over the place."

He leaned forward to ask a question, but I stalled
quickly, remembering to speak up. "And you? What
about you?"

Romney shrugged and ran his finger gingerly around
the edge of his eye patch. "I'm a student at KU. Majoring
in anthropology and archaeology. I was on a neat dig up
in Atchison County near Arrington when I caught a
piece of rock in my eye. That's where I'm coming from
today. The doctor up there said my eye will be okay, but
to be safe he ordered me home for a couple weeks to rest
and give it a chance to heal."

That explained the patch. The swarthy complexion
I'd attributed to his being a "bad" person came from his
being outside in the sun so much. I was too dumb to be
believed, sometimes. I'd nearly been convinced that he
was, if not a mugger, an underground spy. Well, I did get
the underground part somewhat right. "I've always
thought it would be fun to dig up relics, and study history
that way," I said in a moment. I asked, honestly curious,
"How did you get interested in it?"

He stopped eating again. "I was still in high school,
working one summer with an excavation crew digging a
lake." He looked pleased that I'd asked, and he went on
in a voice that seemed warmed, too, by the Kansas sun.
"We don't have many natural lakes back here, most are
man-made. Anyway, we kept turning up artifacts of one
kind and another. Primitive stone implements, pottery,
bones. First I was curious, like anybody. Then I got to
reading a lot about it, and the next thing I knew I was
hooked. Finding out that Kansas has a whole other world

underground just waiting to be dug up, pieced together and studied, fascinated me no end."

"So studying Kansas archaeology is what you plan to do as a career?"

"Oh, no, not just Kansas. I want to travel and study prehistoric cultures in Australia, Melanesia, Polynesia—Africa. The world is my sandbox!" he exclaimed with a grin.

I laughed. "I guess, like your folks, you've traveled a lot?"

He shook his head and gave me a look that made me think of a little baseball-playing kid who has missed an easy pitch he should have caught. A look of unhappy, miserable embarrassment. "I've never been out of Kansas."

What could he be talking about? Maybe money problems, his parents made him stay home so they could go. "How come?" I was curious, but Romney sat cracking his knuckles one by one, saying nothing.

"It's a courage problem," he admitted then, laughing, his face red. "I'm afraid to fly. Stupid, isn't it? But I can't get up the gumption to climb onto one of those big birds. One foot just insists on staying on the ground."

Even though I hadn't been too scared to fly here to Kansas, I thought I knew how he felt. I didn't like Ferris wheels and all those loop-de-loop carnival rides much. "But your career? What will you do, how will you get around?"

"Oh, I'm going to fly," he said flatly. "Eventually, I'll find the nerve." His tone got lighter, and he waved a hand. "I'm working on it all the time. I've got this crazy collection of travel posters tacked on my walls. You should see my room at the farm. Plastered. All these places I'm dying to see are egging me on, from the time I

open my face in the morning. When I get to the satura-
tion point and I can't stand being grounded a moment
longer, I'll fly. And I know it'll be okay." He shrugged.

I believed him, and I felt for him. I had fears of
my own.

I had found Romney Elliot so interesting most of my
sandwich lay uneaten on my plate. I watched him as he
organized his fork and knife on his empty plate and
stuffed his napkin into his empty glass. I liked him, I
decided; at least what I knew of him. He seemed like a
neat guy. So, I would know one person in Greendale.
That was better than going blind into a town where you
didn't know a soul.

In another moment the bus driver was starting to
herd us back to the bus. "Okay if I sit with you?" Rom
asked me with a questioning smile.

I swallowed and then smiled back. "Why not?"

"You haven't been fair, you know," he said when the
bus was rolling again.

"What do you mean?"

"I mean we only talked about me. What about you,
Bryn? Who're you—beyond the lovely face?" I could
barely make out his smile in the gloom of the bus. "What
do you do for fun, what about your hobbies, school,
friends, whatever?"

It wasn't vital information he was asking for and
could hardly bring me problems if I told him. But what
interests could I talk about? Sure, I knew what I'd say if I
could. I'd like to tell him I was an apprentice to a famous
sculptor, say. Or that I had a pilot's license. That I oper-
ated a deep-sea diving bell off the Oregon coast except
on every other weekend when I posed for *Vogue* layouts.
Things to really interest a guy.

It was all I could do to keep from groaning out loud

when I finally admitted, "I read a lot: novels, romances, better things, too. I'm a pretty good cook. Chicken dishes are my specialty, and pies. I've even concocted some low-cal pie recipes all my own that are as tasty as the high-cal ones." I knew none of this could hardly be fascinating to Romney Elliot, and it made me mad that I had to dredge for so little. "I like to go fishing—"

"What?" he exploded with a laugh. "Fishing?"

For some reason, his laughter made me even madder as he turned toward me in the dark. "Yes, fishing. What's wrong with that? I'm darn good, I tell you. I'm not afraid to bait a hook with worms, or herring, or whatever, the way most girls are. That's if I'm bait fishing. I also fish with flies and lures, and I can cast as well as anybody I've seen yet. And I usually get my limit. That's funny?"

"Gosh, no. I like it. You're the first girl I've ever met who looks like a fashion model and likes to go fishing. I think it's just great."

Only I hardly heard him since I was still steaming. "Oregon is known for its great fishing streams, and the ocean, you know. We have trout, trophy-sized, and steelhead and salmon—" I should know what I was talking about. I'd spent a lot of my years on creeks and riverbanks, going after good meals for Gram and me. Then, as quickly as I'd begun, I ran out of vinegar and was simply embarrassed. I leaned away from Romney, against the bus window.

Only he didn't seem to think I was dumb. He turned on the overhead light and faced me, smiling as though I were the eighth marvel of the world. "J like to read, too," he told me. "Mostly adventure novels and nonfiction on stuff like archaeology and anthropology. Can't cook worth a damn. I've always wanted to fish in a place like Oregon. You really do go fishing?"

I nodded. "I'm recently into photography..." I tried to tell him, but Romney was shaking his head, grinning, his mind still stuck on my fishing.

"A girl who looks smashing and who knows how to fish. I can't believe it."

I settled back and let him mull it. I was out of explanations.

THISTLE DOWN HOUSE WAS PROBABLY EVERYTHING Rom said it was. Half-asleep when we got there, I was barely aware of standing in a living room filled with old-fashioned furniture. A small, bespectacled Mr. Gannaway had discussed a room with me and here I was upstairs in a large green and white room sagging against the door, alone. One day's travel felt more like a week's, maybe because I wasn't used to it. I could hardly wait to crawl into bed.

I took out my contact lenses and got ready to shower, recalling the remainder of the bus ride with Rom Elliot. We had talked on for quite a while, mostly comparing Kansas and Oregon. He was plainly proud of his home state, even though I had teased him about the awful heat, tornadoes, and blizzards I'd heard about. He reminded me of Oregon's constant rain, plus the closeness and possible danger of Mount St. Helens' volcano. It had been fun, a good-natured argument, and I smiled to myself, remembering.

I'd felt just fine sitting next to Rom all the rest of the way. When he left me here at Thistle Down House he had asked me if he could see me again while I was here. I guessed it was my polished new look that had caught his attention at first. He liked the idea that I knew how to fish. Maybe to him, I was—what did they call it—an *enigma?* A riddle. Anyway, he was interested. And although that made me feel good, I hadn't answered him, just smiled. If I hadn't been so tired I would probably have come right out and turned him down. I didn't want anything to get in the way of my search here-, not even a guy like Rom. Two weeks wasn't very long to find out what I needed to know.

I felt more awake when I got out of the shower. I dried off, slipped into a lacy nightie, and began to prowl my new space, a large dogwood-flower-papered room with homey comforts. Bed, desk, soft easy chair, cheap TV. Dining table dividing the bed area from the cute kitchenette. Everything was small but neat and tidy. I had my own bathroom and adjoining dressing room, mirrored and wallpapered in soft green and peach stripes.

I went into the kitchen area and began opening the cupboards. I did enjoy cooking. I'd told Rom the truth. I'd talked Gram into letting me do the cooking when I realized her plain, starchy fare was going to have us both as big as houses, eventually. I liked the challenge of fixing dishes that were nutritious and at the same time didn't cost an arm and a leg. I thought Gram was impressed, but I only had her appetite to go by.

The cupboards held a bare minimum of utensils, but for only two weeks I could get by. Mr. Gannaway had said Thistle Down House also had a dining room where I could eat if I wanted.

In the desk drawer, I found stationery, a Bible, and a telephone directory. Pleased with my surroundings, I jumped on the bed like a happy kid, then I remembered Smiley. I'd unpack most of my stuff tomorrow, but Smiley had to come out of my tote. I propped the raggedy clown hand puppet against the brass base of the bedside lamp. He'd been with me for an awfully long time, since second grade when Gram helped me make him from scraps of flannel for a school program.

It would be hard to explain to another adult why I still kept Smiley, but no way could I leave him in Oregon. He was like family, the only one, often, I'd had to talk out my troubles to over the years. He'd helped me over a lot of humps. His wide, red-lipped smile always encouraged, and right now made this room homier, safe.

" 'Night, Smiley," I said. "We did it, didn't we? We're here." I slid between the sheets and knew then the place was well-named. The bed felt heavenly, like thistledown. I would like it here, no problem.

Chapter Three

I woke later than I'd planned the next morning. I was excited as I dressed, even worried, feeling that I was about to make a discovery and find more than the me in the mirror. The real me.

I walked up and down halls and stairways until I finally located the main dining room at the back of the house on the main floor. It appeared that most others staying here were already up and out. A tall, Swedish-looking blonde with a sunny smile introduced herself as Louise, Mrs. Gannaway. Not until I assured her that I'd had a wonderful night's sleep, that the fruit and rolls and tea she brought me were delicious (which they were), did Louise nod in satisfaction and whisk away through a door to the kitchen.

I ate, staring through a window at a small backyard flower and vegetable garden, my mind on how I felt about not having a family. I knew some people might not mind at all, being alone. But I minded. All my life I'd felt a dreadful lack, an aloneness that was hard to deal with. Deep down I hungered for the hugs and kisses, the touch and attention of a mother and father, an aunt, uncle, or anybody related to me who could be proud of me, love me. So far, I'd had only Gram, and she hadn't wanted anybody close to her. I planned to do everything I could to find out if Gram might have relatives here.

The night before leaving Oregon I'd made a fast trip to a nearby bookstore where I bought a booklet called *Tracing Your Roots*. Using tips in it, I planned to make my discoveries. One of the first suggestions was to look in telephone directories for the family surname. I'd done that this morning in my room, before coming down. There wasn't a single Kinney listed in the book, but there were three Joneses, the last name Gram had had when she'd played the organ for movies. It didn't seem possible that I'd find a real clue this soon, but my heart was beating like crazy with hope, just the same.

Folded in the pocket of my jeans was a paper listing the addresses I'd copied from the phone directory. I could hardly wait to follow them up. Finally, unable to swallow another bite, I left the rooming house.

Outside, on the sidewalk, I was surprised it could be so hot this time of morning; the heat was so intense it nearly made me stagger after the Thistle Down's air-conditioned rooms. It was good I'd worn my loose, lavender gauze shirt with my jeans. I started to walk, planning to explore as I went, until I located Elm Street, where the first Jones on my list lived.

As Rom said, it was a nice town. A department store, variety store, restaurants, bookstore, and other businesses you'd find in most towns lined either side of Main Street. As I passed a green-trimmed art shop, I returned the smile of the woman arranging porcelain figurines in the window. She was a sharp-looking lady in dark blue, her black hair pulled back tight in a chignon. Painted on the store window in gilt was: the van orden gallery. Below that: *Watercolors—Sculpture—Collectibles*. All right, I thought, nice place. I'd save it for sightseeing another time.

Maybe the woman could help me. I retraced my steps and entered the art gallery, thankful at once for its cool air. The woman turned from her work at the window. "May I help you find something? Are you looking for a special gift for someone?" For whatever reason, she reminded me of a gorgeous animal, a black panther maybe. Yet despite her cool, sophisticated outward appearance, her smile was open and warm.

I felt foolish as I asked her, barely getting it out, "Could you tell me how to find Elm Street? I'm a little lost."

"I beg your pardon?" she smiled.

I repeated my request, and the woman nodded. "Of course!" She came to rest a hand on my shoulder and led me back to the door. "See the comer there at the end of the block?" She pointed through the window, speaking with a faint accent. "Take that street, it's called Horton, west. Go two more blocks. Elm is well marked, you won't have any trouble."

"Thanks." At a sound behind us, we both turned. A man in a wheelchair that seemed to run itself came from in back of a high counter where sculptured eagles were displayed. I hadn't noticed him till now. He was a thin man with silvery hair and a thick, neatly trimmed mustache. He looked tired and trapped in the chair. I suspected, touched by the way he looked, that I was seeing the remnants of a once-handsome and active man.

"I'm sorry to interrupt, Colette," he said slowly, "but I don't think I want to stay down here at the shop this morning. If you don't mind, I'd like Genevieve to come and get me."

The woman, Colette, nodded. "Definitely, Travis. You mustn't stay if it's tiring you." She started for the telephone, then turned to me, "Is that all, dear?" Her hand, wearing a huge ruby ring, was lifted helpfully. "Is there anything else I can do for you?"

I smiled and shook my head, turning for the door. "Thanks again." I waved to the man in the wheelchair. He waved a narrow hand to me, a lively spark showing for a second in his look.

Emptying my mind of this poor stranger and feeling eager again, I set out, walking quickly down the block to Horton Street.

~

WHEN I REACHED THE FIRST ADDRESS ON MY LIST, I stared at the small white house and then at the scribbled address in my hand at least three times. This was 355 Elm Street, no mistake. Three black children were climbing in a huge tree in the front yard, pulling themselves up to the first big branch by way of a rope swing. I went over to where the earth was bare under the tree and, looking up into the greenery, asked, "Is your name Jones?" I was sure already what the answer would be, but I wanted to be positive.

"Yeah, what's it to you?" a boy about ten called down from where he lay belly down along a branch, snickering.

A girl about eight dropped to the ground in front of me, yelling over her shoulder, "Charles, don't be so snotty." She grinned. "I'm Mary Kim Jones. What did you want?"

I shrugged, feeling misgivings. "I was trying to find

some relatives of mine named Jones, and I hoped they might live here."

Mary Kim giggled, tried to stop, then continued to giggle with her hand over her mouth.

I started to laugh, too. "I know what you're thinking!"

"If you're related to me—" Mary Kim nodded, chortling out loud. "... somebody got the flavors mixed up. 'Cause for sure you're vanilla and I'm chocolate!"

There wasn't much I could say to that. So I asked about the other Joneses listed in the directory. "Chocolate, all chocolate," Mary Kim announced. "My Uncle Thad is one Jones, he lives five blocks over on Meredith Street. Grandma Lucy Jones is the other."

"I thought that might be the case. Thanks, Mary Kim. I'll have to find them some other way if any of my people are here."

MAYBE I WASN'T GOING TO BE SO LUCKY AFTER ALL. I decided to scout the town for a while. I bought a photo album at the drugstore. One thing I knew from the clipping, Gram had lived here in Greendale in the 'Twenties. So I would start an album of pictures of the town. Later, maybe, there would be photographs of people I could add, if I could locate any uncles or cousins or anything. One of the first things I'd bought back in Oregon when I'd found out I had money was a thirty-five-millimeter camera, fully automatic and, I hoped, foolproof.

I spent the afternoon shooting pictures at random. Anything that looked remotely interesting: buildings, trees, signposts. I was getting a shot of the Van Orden Gallery from across the street when the woman named Colette, whom I'd talked with earlier, came out and called over to me, "What are you doing, my dear? Why are you taking pictures of my shop?"

I crossed over and saw that she didn't seem upset, just curious in a friendly way. If this was her shop, then she must be Mrs. Van Orden, Colette Van Orden, and the man in the wheelchair was probably her husband. This ran through my mind while I tried to decide how to answer her. Finally, I shook my head and said, "I really didn't have any special reason for taking a picture of your shop, Mrs. Van Orden. I was getting shots of a little bit of everything around town."

"I thought perhaps you were a magazine writer or newspaper photographer." She sounded a trifle disappointed. Then she added, "I don't know that I've seen you around before, and yet you know who I am?"

"A good guess, that's all. You said this was your shop." I pointed at the gallery window sign. "And yes, I am new in town. But I'm not a writer. Not a photographer, either, although I wouldn't mind being one, someday. I'm just vacationing."

Mrs. Van Orden nodded knowingly. "I've been here for years, and I am acquainted with just about everyone here. Are you staying in town long?"

She was just being nice, and she was easy to talk to, but I wasn't sure how much I wanted to tell her. "I—I'm only here for a couple of weeks, exploring old family stamping grounds. My ancestors might have been from around here." Unable to resist, I decided to take a chance, a long shot.

"My grandmother's name was Ivana Jones Kinney, but she's dead now. Ever hear of her?"

Maybe I only imagined that Colette Van Orden turned a shade whiter. I must have because her smile was unconcerned. "I may have, dear, but at the moment I can't recall. I don't think so. I couldn't have known her well, or I'd remember."

So that was that. Only why did I have the feeling that Mrs. Van Orden was shaken and that she was giving me a thorough going-over while appearing not to? Maybe she was just curious, I thought, and polite. "If you hear of anyone who might have known my grandmother, would you let me know? I'm Bryn Kinney, and I'm staying at the Thistle Down."

THAT SAME NIGHT, MY SECOND IN GREENDALE IF YOU counted my arrival, Rom Elliot telephoned me at Thistle Down House to ask if I'd go with him to the lake the next day. I'd been attracted to him on the bus, no question, and I hadn't quite gotten him out of my mind. So turning him down wasn't easy. But I had to stick with my earlier decision. I'd spent the evening going over my booklet about how to trace family roots, and I'd made up my mind to visit the local cemetery tomorrow. I wanted to look for the names Jones and Kinney on the head-stones. Although it was really living family I was after, the booklet promised that a lot of helpful information could be gotten from tombstones.

Romney sounded disappointed, and I felt a glad little thrill when he said he meant to keep trying. If I *could* squeeze in a date with him before I had to go back to Oregon, I would. I'd love to! In the meantime, though, tracking down information about Gram's past and my own would have to have first priority.

MATTHEW GANNAWAY, THISTLE DOWN OWNER, GAVE me directions to the cemetery when I asked. He was busy at the time, weeding a front-yard flowerbed, and didn't seem to think it was an odd request from one of his guests. I bought an apple at the grocery store, and with my hopes high, I set off, my camera dangling from my shoulder because I wanted to get more pictures.

Once on the edge of town, I could see the cemetery on a knoll to the east, sheltered by a couple of big trees. As far as I looked in every direction, the Flint Hills rose hill upon hill, a mass of green turning to misty blue and then a hazy purple in the far distance. A refreshing view that made me feel washed with happiness all over.

But then, after walking and walking, I came to the conclusion that distance in Kansas is deceiving. I seemed to be getting nowhere; the cemetery was still a long way off. After a while, I demolished my apple and realized it would have been smarter to bring a whole lunch, but it was too late, now, to worry about more food.

I felt hot, sticky, and practically too tired to care when I finally got to the fenced-in graveyard. I crumpled in the shade of a big sycamore tree just inside the gate and found it was only slightly cooler than out in the full sun. For a long time, I leaned back with my eyes closed. Finally, I had to admit that I was stalling, putting off the chance for disappointment. I had no guarantee that an ancestor of mine lay here. And I wanted so badly to find something.

Still sitting, I opened my eyes and began to read the carved messages on the nearer tombstones. It was an old-fashioned cemetery that dated back a hundred years, by the dates on some stones. And, too, the gravemarkers were a variety of shapes and sizes, not uniformly flat to the ground like most stones in modem cemeteries. I decided these monuments with etched vines and flowers and sentimental sayings held more interest for me.

Written on one stone was "Resting at Home." And on
another: "She Was a Good and Noble Woman." Then,
"Farewell 'Til We Meet on the Banks of That Beautiful
River," and "Another Link Is Broken in Our Household
Band, But a Chain Is Forming in a Better Land."

I had my energy back so there was no excuse to put
off my mission any longer. I got to my feet, and following
a plan I'd decided on while sitting, I made my way among
the stones, row by row, stopping to read each one, just
the names. It seemed to take forever. The sun felt fierce
on my head, but I had no intention of quitting until I'd
read them all, every last stone.

I wanted to cry in disappointment as I wandered the
cemetery up and down without seeing a single Kinney
marker and not even a Jones, which was so common. It
wasn't fair! I'd come so far, and I was gaining *zero*. Finally,
I'd read every monument from the south fence to the
north, east to west. There was nothing here! I might as
well start the walk back to Greendale. I sighed, not
looking forward to that jaunt in the heat of the afternoon. I started to make my way around a tangled, weedy
clump of purple iris, and in that second, spotted a small
marker nearly buried in the plants. A marker I'd missed
the first time around.

On my knees I made out the name carved in large
lettering on the stone: jones. I could hardly breathe as I
crouched there, brushing the dried grasses and iris back
from the monument for a better look. Besides being
small, the stone was plainer than many of them. The
wording was small and hard to make out. In a whisper, I
sounded it out:

*"Gamble Jones. Age 22 Approximately. Died This Day,
September 20, 1924. Beloved Husband of Ivana Jones. Flame of
Her Heart, Light of Her life."*

My heart tightened further and seemed to stop. I sat back on the ground hard. A tide of emotion swept over me, and I couldn't help swaying as I sat with my forehead on my knees, sobbing. I'd found something! I'd found something for true. I'd hoped to, but I didn't really believe I would, I realized now.

Poor Gram, to lose her husband so young. Only twenty-two! So now I knew that Jones was not Gram's maiden name, but the name of her husband when she married, probably the first time.

Her name was still Jones when she went off to play the organ for picture shows, according to the clipping. So Kinney, the movie man, had to've come into her life after that.

And where did I fit in? What took place over all those years? Who married who? Were there other children besides me, and to whom were they born? What about family get-togethers and funny family stories and family traditions? Why was there this big secret, this big blank space in my past? I couldn't stand not knowing anything.

Chapter Four

I wiped at tears that wouldn't stop, picked up my camera, and on one knee I took a picture of the monument. Through the viewfinder, I saw how dumpy the grave was. Which showed there was no one close to take care of it, or at least to care. I cared. I wiped my face on my sleeve once more and lay the camera aside. I yanked out the dead grass around the marker, making a pile of the grass and adding to it the faded iris blooms that I snapped off one by one.

My grandmother—and I hoped she truly was my grandmother because if she was, further answers might come easier now—had no doubt planted the iris with her own young woman's hands years ago. The clumps had multiplied, some dying out, others living on, like a family.

I no longer felt the heat or the weariness in my legs from the long walk. I did what I could, then resolved that I would come back with tools another time and do the job right.

When I finally looked up, I saw by the sun that a lot more time had passed than I was aware of. It must be three o'clock, maybe later. Time to get back to town. Off to the right, a glittering bit of movement caught my attention. Looking, I saw a silver-colored late-model car pull slowly away from the cemetery gate, maybe seventy-five yards from where I squatted. I got to my feet for a better look, shading my eyes, and saw that the driver seemed to be staring at me, and why? Or was the person really concerned with me?

The person behind the wheel looked like Mrs. Van Orden from the shape of the head, but again I couldn't be sure. Mrs. Van Orden must have come to mind because I'd been talking to her only this morning. Whatever, the car was leaving.

IT WAS A SMALL SURPRISE WHEN IT SEEMED TO TAKE hours to get back to Greendale. But as I grew closer to town, I had a feeling of coming home. Ironic, since I'd only been here a couple of days. It would be great to get back to my place, take a shower, and fix a good, nourishing dinner. The only thing I'd eaten since breakfast was the apple. At least I didn't have to worry about those awful fourteen pounds coming back.

I reached Second Street thinking "Only one more block to go" when I saw a familiar-looking guy getting out of a car at the curb in front of a restaurant across the way. A restaurant called the Garden Party. Rom! I walked faster, all set to yell at him when I saw the door on the passenger side open and a girl get out. A small, blond, cuddly-looking girl in a white skirt and baby blue top.

My heart just seemed to drop out of me. Not only that, I suddenly felt elephant-sized, dirty, and ugly. I prayed Rom wouldn't see me, but he turned, saw me and yelled, "Hey, Bryn!" I waved, but that wasn't enough for him. He came running across the street to meet me, a wide smile on his tan face. "My friend and I are about to have something cool at the Garden Party, local oasis." He motioned with his head. "Why don't you join us?"

I made an effort to pretend there was no grime under my fingernails, no dust on my jeans, and that my hair wasn't as tangled as a bird's nest. The blonde was waiting by the car, watching us. From this distance, I couldn't guess her mood, but I couldn't imagine any girl wishing to share Romney Elliot. I shook my head and adjusted the camera bag strap, which was cutting into my shoulder. "I'd like to, but I've been on a long hike and I'm bushed. I think I'll have a shower and a quick meal in my room. It's been a long day. Thanks anyway, Rom."

Under his furry brow, his uncovered eye examined my face longer than was comfortable, and his smile was puzzled. Then he heaved a sigh. "Maybe next time. Have you been taking pictures of the good old Flint Hills? I guess they don't compare with all that scenic beauty you've got in Oregon, but they're not bad, are they? You're having a good time?"

I felt my head bobbing like Smiley's as I nodded to each question. I wished he'd go back to *his friend* and leave me be. There were things I needed to think about, plans I had to make. "Uh, Rom, I have to go. But it was great—nice— seeing you," I mumbled.

"Sure." He shrugged.

I watched him cross the street, wide-shouldered, hands in his pockets. I felt glum, robbed, and resentful. Which made no sense, because I was making the choices.

I was really dragging when I got to the Thistle Down. Upstairs, I jumped into the shower and after a long time still didn't want to get out. I did feel better, later, clean and dressed. I went out to the nearest supermarket for the makings of a chef salad, milk, and cereal for the morning, and sandwich fixings for after that.

It was late when I finished dinner. I got into my nightgown and crawled onto my bed to read *Tracing Your Roots*. I could see that the job would be easier if I had more details to go on than just names: my own, Bryn Kinney, Gram's, which was Ivana Jones Kinney, and her young husband's who'd died, Gamble Jones. Beyond that, I knew only that Gram had lived here and had gone out from here to play the organ for movies. Not much information when you thought about it. Someway, though, I'd find out the rest. Tomorrow I intended to take a bus to Cottonwood Falls, the county seat according to Mr. Gannaway. I'd look into old court records there.

Close to sleep that night, I thought how great it would be if there was a place you could go to and say, "Excuse me, but my past is missing," and get all the answers you wanted. But it was a foolish, hopeless wish. It was going to take more than that to learn what I wanted.

FOR HOURS AND HOURS THE NEXT DAY, AFTER I'D BEEN directed to the Cottonwood Falls courthouse, I thumbed through heavy ledgers provided to me. You couldn't call looking things up one of my passions; I'd never liked it. Today I thought my eyes would fall out reading the musty old record books, looking for a familiar name. It didn't please me, either, to know that while I drudged away here, Rom no doubt was keeping cool at the lake with the cute blonde. Again I had to remind myself that my choices were my own doing.

Yet, though the booklet said I'd find a wealth of information in old records of births, divorces, deaths, deeds, wills, and so on, I began to wonder if that were true. I didn't expect to find a record of my own birth, since that was supposedly sealed away somewhere, but I had hoped to find some record of Gram's or Gamble Jones's. But whatever else had happened before in my family, it must have been recorded in a different county, possibly a different state, which left me at a loss.

I considered, too, that the information was there and I was missing it. Looking up local records sounded easier to me. Maybe I could find a record of Ivana and Gamble's marriage in Greendale, perhaps at a Justice of the Peace as the book mentioned.

I felt defeated at the end of the day, riding the bus back to Greendale. Not that I would allow it to get me down. There were other things I could do. I'd already asked Colette Van Orden if she knew of Gram, without results. It was time to forget caution and ask anybody and everybody who'd listen. Someone living in Greendale must have known Gram in the old days and could tell me things.

I doubt if I hadn't been so desperate, that I would have had the nerve to go door to door, business to business, the way I did the next day, asking people if they had ever heard of my grandmother, Ivana Jones Kinney. As it was, some pretty odd looks were thrown my way. Not from Mr. Gannaway and his wife Louise, the ones I started with. But they had only been in Greendale for five years, so of course they hadn't heard of her. No one else had known Gram, either. Most of the residents I talked to hadn't been here very long, about ten to fifteen years, many of them.

I cornered a pair of really elderly men sitting on a bench in the town square, but one of them was so hard of hearing I couldn't make him understand what it was I wanted. The other was so senile he thought I was his granddaughter coming to take him home to lunch, and it was a fight to get him to stay where he was and not follow me.

ANOTHER DAY I WENT ABOUT TOWN CONTACTING THE president of each local club and organization like the D.A.R., Eastern Star Lodge, church guilds, and so on. Gram wasn't listed on a single membership roster, which didn't surprise me. The Gram I'd known for sure hadn't been a joiner. If there was a listing for hermits, though, I may have found her name.

It crossed my mind that people might be getting tired of me, thinking I was a pest. But my time here would be up at the end of next week. It was laughable that back in Oregon I'd imagined that I'd be throwing my arms about long-lost relatives by this time.

I still wanted to see if Greendale had a Justice of the Peace, one who hung onto old records. If fate was on my side at all, Gram and Gamble maybe at least tied the knot here in Greendale. Such listings, according to my booklet, occasionally gave roots information, like the names of parents of the bride and groom, birthplaces, and names of witnesses. The right record could point me in the right direction and turn out to be invaluable. So I had to keep at it.

A QUICK CHECK OF THE TELEPHONE DIRECTORY THE next day showed no Justice of the Peace listed. Discussing the fact, later, with Mrs. Van Orden, one of the town's older residents, I found that Justice of the Peace had been phased out of the Kansas judicial system some fifteen years earlier. Old records might have been turned over to the county, she thought.

I was so disgusted when Colette asked if it was important, I snapped back that it sure was to me—which caused her to bridle a bit as she went back to work dusting a shelf of oriental vases. Of course, none of this was her fault. I apologized all over the place and left, still feeling guilty for pestering her.

Agitated over the whole thing, I tried reading for a while in my room, but I couldn't keep my mind on the words. I redid my nails. Later, I turned on the small TV, but I couldn't get interested in *All My Children,* either. If I didn't do something, my stay in Greendale was going to be a total waste.

The *schools*—it hit me over a sandwich lunch. Yearbooks would be great information! It would be fun to see a picture of Grandma when she was in high school if she'd attended. She might have, or maybe Gamble did. Now that I had a fresh idea, I could hardly contain my excitement.

Judging from Gram's age when she died, 79, she would have been seventeen or eighteen around 1922 or 1923. Did yearbooks exist then? It was worth a try to find out!

It was summer vacation, naturally, and I didn't expect anyone to answer at the high school, but I found the number and dialed it just in case. After a dozen echoing rings, I put the receiver back on the hook and ran downstairs. I couldn't find either of the Gannaways on the premises, maybe they were at the store or something. But I had to find out who the high school principal was because if I could find him at home he could maybe let me in the school to look at the yearbooks. I dreaded bothering Mrs. Van Orden again, but maybe one more question wouldn't hurt. I headed for the art gallery.

If she was still put out with me, Colette Van Orden didn't show it; rather, she was all patient as she spoke in her intriguing voice, "Mica Davidson is the high school principal, dear. But everyone in town knows him as Dave." She smiled.

"Thanks!" I was dying to be on my way, but out of politeness, I pretended interest in a watercolor of a child in a swing that hung on the wall. The next thing I knew, Colette was saying, "I don't know what you want of Dave, but he and his family are on vacation in California."

"What?" I almost shrieked, "On vacation in California? But I need to get into the high school to see their collection of yearbooks."

"My goodness!" Mrs. Van Orden laughed. "Why would you want to do that?"

Exasperated, I told her, "My grandmother. I think I mentioned the other day that she may have been from around here. And—and I'm just curious—about her—when she was young. I guess it really isn't important." Only it was, very important. I was struck by another idea. "Hey, maybe someone on the school board could let me into the school? Who is the president of the school board?" All at once I was revved up again with hope.

But Mrs. Van Orden was slow to answer, looking as though she wasn't sure, or more that she was reluctant to say, which didn't make any sense. "Alice Jennings," she murmured finally.

"Would she be listed in the phone book under her name or her husband's?"

Her mouth seemed to tighten a bit, but she told me, "Alice will be listed as Mrs. Bill Jennings."

This time I was deeply embarrassed and felt guiltier than ever. "Look, Mrs. Van Orden, I'm really sorry for bothering you, but this means a lot to me. Here you have such a nice place and all I ever do is bother you with questions. But I'm going to buy something. Before I go back to Oregon, I want to get a super-special souvenir to take back with me. All right? I really do appreciate your help."

She was all graciousness, her warm smile in place. "It's nothing, dear. And please don't think you're a bother. If I seem impatient, if I'm not myself, it's because of Travis, my husband. He isn't well, and I worry about him. I—I'd die if anything happened to him, he means so much to me." A sparkle of tears showed in her eyes, and I felt worse. This problem with her husband's health was all the more reason why I shouldn't bother her; she had enough on her mind. I slipped from the gallery feeling like a rotten egg.

Well, I would buy the biggest statue from her that I could carry back on the plane, I decided on the way to my room at Thistle Down House. Our exchange had left me with a terribly dry throat, so I made myself a tall glass of iced tea before I got comfortable by the phone. As I flipped through the directory to find the telephone number for Mrs. Alice (Bill) Jennings, school board president, Smiley beamed good luck at me from his station by the lamp. I dialed.

In reply to my request to see the school's yearbooks, Alice Jennings came crisply to the point, "For what reason may I ask?"

"Well," I stammered as something seemed to stick in my throat, "I—I would just like to, because—"

"Without good reason," she interrupted, "we can't do

it. Surely you understand. We can't open up the school for just anyone."

I wanted to scream at her, "I'M NOT JUST ANYONE. I'm Bryn Anne Kinney, and my grandma, Ivana, lived here and her first husband, Gamble, is buried here, and I have a right, that's all!" Except I wasn't sure I had a right, so I said nothing.

Evidently, no excuse would have been good enough, because on the other end of the line, Mrs. Jennings was saying, "I'm sorry, Miss, but I can't do what you ask. If Dave, our principal, were available, he might give you another answer. But he's out of town, and I won't do this." With that, she hung up.

Rude!

For hours afterward, I was too angry to think, too upset to do anything but pace furiously back and forth in my room, ranting at fate, at the roadblocks that continued to stand in my way. Finally, my fury burned out, I fell asleep with Smiley in my arms.

Chapter Five

The next day I visited the building that housed the local *Greendale Bulletin* newspaper. Unfortunately, the drooping, thin-voiced editor told me, the building was not large enough to hold a back file of old newspapers. I had it in mind to search newspapers from the 1922 to 1924 period for a possible account of Gram's and Gamble Jones's marriage. Gamble had died in 1924, so he and Ivana would have had to have married before that. The years 1922 to 1924 would be a good guess. For some reason, I didn't have a lot of hope of finding anything; maybe I was getting used to disappointment. But I went to the library anyway, where the editor said old papers were kept.

I was ushered into a side room where endless shelves of yellowing newspapers made me shudder to think of a search through them. Thankfully, the library aide had segregated the years I was looking for, for me. Thumbing the pages gingerly, I saw that few photographs were used with wedding stories in those days. Instead, a small drawing of wedding bells marked the column of wedding notices on each paper.

It simplified matters to turn each time to the wedding bells symbol, even so, I was getting bored with the whole thing when I saw what I was looking for. The tiny account, hardly two inches square, leaped out at me as if it were written in bold headlines:

"July 10, 1924, at 10 a.m. Miss Ivana Burgess, age 19, was married to Gamble Jones, age 22, in a simple ceremony before the local court judge, Stanfield Johanson," it began.

I trembled as I got out my pen and notebook to copy the story; inside I was quivering worse. The story noted that it was the first marriage for both. Parents mentioned for Ivana Burgess, Gram, were Homer Burgess, living, and Rosemary Burgess, deceased. That was in 1924, of course. No parents were mentioned for Gamble. Witnesses to the ceremony were friends of the bride and groom, Maryanna Lawson and George Glenn.

Gram's first marriage; I had it! I got up right there and danced to wild and soundless music. I now knew Gram's maiden name, Burgess. The names of her parents, *my* great-grandparents: Rosemary and Homer Burgess. I had the names of witnesses, but thinking further, I knew Gram's friends were possibly her age or older. They might be dead. They might have moved from here. Still, I could look for the names in the telephone directory.

My feet were still practically dancing as I flew out of the library and down the street toward Thistle Down House. Then, unable to wait, I ducked into a telephone booth on the way, for a look at the directory. A few minutes of thumbing showed no Lawson listed, nor a George Glenn. Maryanna Lawson could have changed her name by marrying. Any of them could have moved. Sixty years was a long time ago. I looked for Stanfield Johanson, the Justice of the Peace who had performed the ceremony, but he wasn't in the book, either. I wasn't too disappointed. I had at least found something more to go on.

To my surprise, there was a letter for me on the hall table when I got back to Thisde Down House. Sure it was from Rom, I raced upstairs to read it. By the time I'd flopped on my bed, my heart was leaping crazily. I tore the envelope open, but it wasn't from Rom. A cold chill ran like a zipper up my spine as I read the neatly typed message:

I know who you are and why you are here. Don't make trouble!! Leave, now!

I reread the note, and the chill moved to the pit of my stomach. I was overwhelmed with the urge to throw my things in my suitcase and just *go*. The hate I read between the lines made me feel sick, and creepy all over. Then I got mad.

"After all," I told Smiley, cuddled in my arms, "nobody has a right to tell me to leave Greendale. I'm not doing anything wrong! I've found out a few innocent details about my grandmother's life. How could that possibly hurt anybody? I'm supposed to scurry back to Oregon like a scared puppy because somebody is afraid I'll find out their deep, dark secrets or something? No way!"

My little clown was grinning "Right on!" at me. If the note writer wanted me to go badly enough, whoever it was could come out and tell me why I should. Otherwise, I was staying.

I couldn't guess who might have written the note. I thought of Colette Van Orden, owner of the art gallery. I was sure I'd rankled her with my many questions, but that was hardly a reason to throw me out of town. I had talked to so many people, asking about Gram. Business people and others around town, the courthouse clerks at Cottonwood Falls, not to mention the president of the school board, Alice Jennings. And any of them could have told others. Anyone could have written the note; the note could even be a joke, although I felt it wasn't.

I had to admit I was scared, and suddenly I knew I had to talk this over with someone. Romney Elliot seemed the only likely possibility, the only one I might trust.

When he answered the phone, I tried to sound calm. "Rom, this is Bryn Kinney. Are you busy?"

"Nan. I was just being lazy in the hammock out back, listening to some tapes. What's up?"

"Could you meet me somewhere right away?"

"Hey, Bryn, I thought you'd never ask!" Joy was mixed with surprise in his voice. "Where, when? Name it."

"It doesn't matter to me, but—the Garden Party Restaurant? Fifteen minutes?"

"Done. See you there."

I WAS WAITING AT A CORNER TABLE WHEN ROM WALKED in, dressed in white trousers and a purple polo shirt. He threaded his way toward me through potted palms and hanging greenery. His grin reflected the gladness I was feeling. "Hi," I said when he sat down.

"Hi, yourself. Excuse my crazy state. I can't believe my good luck today."

I decided to explain right away. "This isn't really a date, Rom. Anyway, the blonde you were here with the other day—?"

"A friend," he shrugged. "I've known Lisa since we were in diapers. We went all through school together.

When we're both home, we try to get together at least once to hash over old times. She's just a friend," he repeated. "Now, you. If this isn't a date, what is it? I thought maybe you wanted to take me fishing."

I half smiled and shook my head. "I need help," I confessed. "But first I want to tell you why I'm here in Greendale, really." He nodded, his expression curious, and I began. I told him the whole story, about Gram's denial of the existence of my parents, and the closed adoption records. How I hadn't known where Gram lived before Oregon, if she was my real grandmother. That I knew nothing about her childhood, or my own babyhood —family.

"I've always felt...incomplete," I tried to explain, "without family. Not knowing anything about them. When Gram died, and I found the clipping mentioning Greendale, the same town listed on my birth registration card, and there was money to do something about it, I knew I had to come here. It was as though the time was right for me to know the answers. It's crazy, but I had the idea I'd come here and find relatives the first day: aunts, uncles, cousins, the whole bit. My mother and father, too, although that seemed a lot to hope for."

"You haven't found anyone?" He leaned toward me, a genuine expression of concern on his face, which made me feel glad I'd spilled everything to him. I was lucky that he, practically a stranger, cared.

"I—I found a grave, a marker. I've uncovered a little information here and there. If only I knew of someone really old to talk to, someone who has lived here for fifty or sixty years and may have known Gram . . . now ..." My voice gave way, and I couldn't finish.

"Now, what?" Rom prompted gently.

My chin trembled as I drew the note from my shirt

pocket and passed it to him, "Now th-this."

"Good God!" he exclaimed when he'd read it. "What bull!"

"I don't know if I should be scared or not," I confessed, half laughing. "Evidently someone is afraid I'm about to rattle a skeleton in their family closet."

He shook his head and read the note again. "I wouldn't worry; it's just some flake being cute. I can see why it would bother you, but don't be scared. For one thing, whoever wrote this didn't actually make any threats of physical harm or anything." He caught my hand across the table, smiling. "Anyhow, no one has a right to bully you, try to make you leave. Any ideas who wrote it, so I can go flatten them?"

Mrs. Van Orden came to mind a second time. "Rom, what do you know about Mrs. Van Orden, the lady who runs the art gallery?"

"You think she sent the note?"

"I don't know. No, I don't think so." My eyebrows felt knotted, but I couldn't help being confused, worried, nor could I keep the strain from my voice. "I can't think why she would. But I am curious about her, Rom."

"Mrs. Van Orden, hmm? Gosh, she's been here all my life; I guess I should know something about her. Let's see — she's married to that guy in the wheelchair, Travis Van Orden, right? Don't see much of him, except when they are together at some town social function. Yeah, I do know that the lady is 'highly respected' as they say. In a way, she helps run the town. Spends money on things like the senior citizen center; a playground for kids. A busy lady. I'm sure her name is on the board of directors of half the civic and philanthropic groups in the county." He sighed. "I'm not making her sound like much of a villain, am I?"

"It's all right. I'm sure she had nothing to do with the note, anyway." I shook my head. I believed that Colette wasn't a native Kansari, even though Rom said she'd been here as long as he could remember. Her accent told me she possibly came from Europe, and that she hadn't been here long enough to be connected with Gram or me, anyway. Someone else must have written the note. Who, or why, I couldn't fathom.

But trying to puzzle it out was giving me a headache; I needed a break, a rest, from this constant pursuit of my past. "The note is no doubt a meaningless bunch of nonsense," I told Rom, "and here we are wasting time over it. Let's change the subject, all right?" I thought about the girl I'd seen him with; I was still curious. "Are you sure Lisa isn't a girlfriend?" I asked, "Or maybe there's someone else?" Of course, this was none of my business, but I hoped he'd tell me.

I watched Rom's face as he grew thoughtful, a grin playing at the corners of his mouth. "There was a girl," he admitted, "a girl really important to me. *Pam.* We were quite a combo the last two years; I figured we'd eventually get married. It didn't pan out."

I guessed from his voice that he still struggled with feelings not quite resolved. "I'm sorry," I said.

Still not looking at me, Rom went on, speaking slowly as he tore a paper napkin into shreds, "Pam was a student at KU, too. She went to Europe over spring break. Decided not to come back. Can you beat that? Gave up school, *me,* her country even, for some doddering Frenchman."

"Honest?" I could hardly believe it. I pictured a lovely girl (she'd have to be pretty to deserve Rom in the first place) with a snowy-haired old man.

Rom nodded. "I heard he's at least thirty-two years

old."

"Rom, thirty-two isn't doddering," I said, trying not to laugh out loud at him when he looked so serious.

"Well, hell!" he exclaimed, starting to crack his knuckles. "I have to find some fault with him, don't I? He stole my girl. And all I know about him other than his age is that he's in banking and drives a Ferrari. Those aren't attributes I like to count."

I had to laugh, then, feeling an unexplainable glee that Pam had gone for the Frenchman when I should have been sorry for Rom. I grabbed his hands, partly to stop his knuckle from cracking, but more because I suddenly had to touch him. He looked at me, as surprised as I was. "How about you? I hope there isn't some guy waiting for you back in Oregon, maybe more than one?"

I took my hands from Rom's, hardly knowing how to answer him. Over the years I'd had a few "sort-of" boyfriends, nothing remotely serious. For one thing, Gram hated to have other people around. That made a real boyfriend thing impossible. And, maybe I wasn't exactly plain back in those days, but I didn't look as finished as I did now, either. "Nobody special in Oregon," I told Rom.

My pulse danced at his responding grin of relief. "Thanks for the good news." If I wasn't careful, I cautioned myself, I could get carried away with Rom. And I couldn't let that happen; not with so much to do in so little time.

Rom might have been reading my mind as he put down his Pepsi and asked, "Have you thought about sticking around in Kansas longer than two weeks? You should. And maybe I can help with your project. Have you located where your grandmother lived when she was here?"

"I've given a little thought to staying on, but I don't want to if I don't have to. And no, I don't have an address here for a house where Gram might have lived. I don't know how to look."

He was eager. "Give me her name again. A lot of the old places around here are known by the name of the original owner. They call them the Lardner place, or the Jackson home, the old Harris ranch, like that."

"Really? Great idea. Gram's full name would have been Ivana Burgess Jones Kinney." I strung them out carefully. "Any of those names ring a bell?"

I could see he wanted to help, but he shook his head. "Sorry, Bryn. I've never heard of a Burgess place, or a Jones, or Kinney. And I thought sure we were onto something that'd help you."

"It doesn't matter." I sat back. "I'm getting used to blind alleys. And—in a way, I'm afraid of the *reason* I'm having trouble finding out things, like maybe I'm not supposed to know, would be better off if I didn't. There was the note—"

"Hey," Rom protested gently, "don't let this get you down. There doesn't necessarily have to be some terrible skeleton rattling in the family closet. I've heard of brothers or father and son, disagreeing over some moot point and then not speaking to each other for years, they got so mad. That may be all there is to it, in your case."

He made me feel much better. I was glad he had put into words a possibility that I'd only vaguely considered. But I wanted to explain *myself.* "Part of the problem is that knowing so little about yourself, who you are, is scary. So far, I have no proof that Gram and I were actually related, beyond the fact that she was my legal guardian. I don't know for sure if Kinney is my real surname, the last name I was born with."

Rom made a soft, sympathetic noise, and he shook his head. "It's hard for me to picture how it is with you because I have a great family. Oh, not that I haven't had the usual problems, but my parents and I are friends now; I like 'em. I wish I knew better how you feel; I do want to help, Bryn. I'll back you up in any way that you need me. I think you should see this through and not let anything stop you."

I swallowed against the lump in my throat. "Thanks. At times I feel like I'm chasing ghosts," I confessed, "and the ghosts seem a whole lot smarter than me. It helps to know you agree with me, that I should keep on."

For a second or two neither of us said anything, and then suddenly, Rom struck the table with his palm. "Birdella Lamb!" he exclaimed, his face lit with discovery.

"What on earth is a birdella lamb?" I asked him, wiping my eyes.

"She's a who, not a what. This has been in the back of my mind ever since you said you needed to talk to a really old-time resident of Greendale. Birdella is ancient, maybe nearly a hundred, and she's lived here most of her life, I think. For years she was a correspondent, sending Greendale, Rington, and Mumford news to the big city papers. If anybody knows anything about the old-timers from around here, she does. You've got to talk to her, Bryn. Sure..." He laughed, clasping his hands in the sign of a winner. "...little old Birdella."

"Gosh, Rom, this is great. I don't know how to thank you!"

"I do," he said promptly. "Go to the lake with me tomorrow."

That stopped me. I'd used up six whole days already. Now that I knew about Birdella Lamb, I wanted to talk to her right away. She could turn out to be my most helpful lead. On the other hand, I owed Rom. And I wanted to be with him. "All right," I agreed, flashing a grin right back at him, "it's a date." Then I remembered that a swimsuit was one item of clothing I hadn't brought with me. I told Rom.

"We'll buy one. Let's go get one right now." Rom stood up and caught my hand in his as I got to my feet. I liked having him hold my hand. And now that we'd finally settled on a date, it was what I wanted most in the world.

For some reason, I didn't mind showing Rom the suits as I tried them on, and after a lot of discussion, we picked a red one. I was just thankful I'd dieted in the spring and underneath all the pudge I'd found bones, rather nice bones. Rom didn't know about the transformation, but he looked pleased with the new me, slim and feminine.

We swam in the lake for hours the next day, taking time out now and then to sun on a floating raft, then fish awhile. My only catch was a huge turtle that sent Rom into spasms of laughter, and I swore to get even. He tried to make up to me by praising my swim strokes. I decided against telling him I'd learned how, alone, in a muddy irrigation ditch in Oregon. Strictly unglamorous.

Toward evening, we got into our clothes and drove into town for dinner. Then we went back for a long, moon-washed canoe ride around the lake. I wanted it to last forever; off in the distance someone's transistor was playing mostly Lionel Ritchie love songs, and it was all very romantic. Rom gave me my first man-woman kiss (man-woman to my mind). Quite a few kisses, truthfully. With no trouble, I knew I could get addicted. Being with Rom made my trip from Oregon worth it if nothing else good happened.

Chapter Six

The day after my date with Rom, I still felt exhilarated, as if I'd been shot with a new kind of happiness. But I'd had a ridiculous nightmare in the night in which I was graduating from college and they were giving me a degree in Fantastic Photography. My newly found parents and tons of relatives looked on, smiling with big red clown lips. It wasn't a regular graduation because I was wearing a wedding dress, and Rom was lifting my veil and kissing me as I got my degree!

I was both embarrassed and happy as I headed to see Birdella Lamb, the old woman Rom had told me about. He'd given me her address.

When I reached the tiny white house, I knocked several times. Finally, I heard the rustle of movement from inside. After a pattering of footsteps, the door opened. A tiny woman stood there, her heavy-lidded, pale blue eyes peering up at me from behind wire-rimmed glasses that looked too large. I asked her, "Miss Lamb? Do you think I might talk to you for a while?"

A fragile, quivery-looking little ancient, she munched on a hot dog while she sized me up. For whatever reason, I felt an immediate liking for the woman. I smiled and repeated, "Birdella Lamb?"

"Eh?"

"I'm looking for Miss Birdella Lamb?"

"I'm Birdella. What d'ya want?" she quaked. "You bring churchy papers? Never mind, I like comp'ny so you can come in, anyway." She tottered off, motioning me to follow. I went along, feeling like a giant following a troll. Although it smelled very old, the house was otherwise a tidy nest. I crossed to a couch and eased down to sit on the edge. My mouth was open to state my case, but Birdella threw me off when she asked, "Wanna hot dog?" The rest of hers went into her mouth, and she chewed complacently.

"No, thanks, I came to—" I tried again, but she interrupted, "A glass of grape juke? I made it myself from my own grapes, from that vine you saw wrapped around my front porch. The juice is ice cold."

"Yes, please." I decided to relax and take my time. "Grape juice sounds wonderful." We'd play by her rules.

"Come in the kitchen, then," Birdella muttered, flitting off. "I don't want you spilling on my couch."

I obeyed. The sunny kitchen was hardly more than an alcove attached to the rest of the house. I took one of two chairs at the table and, in a moment, tried again. "I'm here to find out about my grandmother, my ancestors, if possible—" She hadn't heard me, I could tell. Besides being probably hard of hearing, Birdella was making a lot of noise getting glasses from the cupboard and juice from the fridge, and banging doors.

Birdella poured the juice and brought napkins. My napkin looked used, and it was decorated with silver

wedding bells and the names, Joe and Nancy. I looked at
Birdella's and saw that it was decorated with autumn
leaves. "Aren't they pretty?" Birdella crowed, holding hers
up. "I save all the pretty napkins I get from weddings,
funerals, and such. Now, go ahead and talk to me about
Jesus."

"You don't understand." I shook my head, a little
worried that I might not be able to get through to her at
all. "I'm not here from a church. I understand that you've
lived in Greendale or near here, for a long time. You must
have known many people who've come and gone. I'm
here to find out if you knew Ivana Burgess?"

Birdella stared back at me as if I was half-witted or
something. " 'Course I knew Ivana. She was Rosemary's
and Homer's daughter."

"Yes!" I cried, astonished—although maybe I
shouldn't have been. "Rosemary's and Homer's daughter.
You knew them? You knew Ivana? What can you tell me
about her? I think Ivana was my grandmother, but she's
no longer living so..." The blood was rushing to the top
of my head, I was so excited.

"It wasn't Ivana's fault that she ended up without a
dime," Birdella quavered. "It was Homer's. It was her pa's
fault. But you and I both know Homer only did what he
thought best. I don't fault him for it, do you?"

I had no idea what she meant. "Wait a minute," I
begged, smiling at her, "let's keep this straight. Would
you rather talk about Homer, first? He was Ivana's father,
that's true." And probably *my* great-grandfather, I
reminded myself silently.

"Homer was personable," Birdella's voice came softly.
From the bashful, sweet expression on her pruny little
face, the woman had had quite a crush on my great-
grandfather, I felt.

"What else about Homer?"

"He was a rural mail carrier, but everybody knows that. Carried mail by horse and buggy all around these parts. If Rosemary hadn't nabbed him, I would have." Birdella looked away, sniffling a bit.

"Tell me about Rosemary," I urged, wanting to hear about my great-grandmother.

"Oh, her. She was plain, and there ain't no use to fib about that. Plain as a post. She was born a Halic, remember? All them Halics was plain, excepting Selena."

Whoa, my mind ordered. Two more names to remember: Halic was my great-grandmother's maiden name! And there was Selena, whoever she was. My heart was thudding in my ears, and yet I didn't want to miss a word. I'd thought of bringing a tape recorder or notebook and pen, but I'd been afraid Birdella wouldn't talk as freely if I did. "And...?" I coaxed gently, taking a sip of my grape juice.

Birdella struck the table with her tiny fist, "Those Halics had more money than is good for people, anyhow, and Homer, he knew it. Rich, they were. From wheat ranching"—she ticked off on a finger—"and oil, and cattle." Her eyes narrowed as she went on. "Rosemary liked the cattle best. She was always on the back of a horse, out with the men, working with them cows. I don't like to say it, but she was a great horsewoman, give her that."

"That's nice. I mean—it's so great to hear all this." I spoke hurriedly, anxious for her to go on, but for the moment Birdella seemed wrapped in thought, her mind far away.

"If I'd known what Rosemary was doing, I could have beat her time," Birdella reflected in a flat voice, a peevish look on her face. "You heard what Rosemary did? She was meeting Homer when he was making his rounds with the mail! Right out on the road, they'd stop and pass the time of day, and spoon a little, too, would be my guess. Oh, maybe it was true love; I know it was, 'cause you remember, Homer was a simple man, just a mail carrier. She had money, but she was awful plain, too. They were a fair match, in a way..." Her voice trailed off and she stared at empty space. I was sure she'd forgotten I was there.

Then she went on suddenly, as if to herself, "Rosemary was a good person, much as I hate to think it. Oughtn't to hold it against her 'cause she got the beau I wanted. She'd do for anybody, a kind soul. Homer must have loved her for herself. He sure didn't marry her for her money; he hated it. You might say he married her in spite of her money. He was afraid of money, you know."

"But why?" I asked. I was hearing so much, finally, about *my* people, at least Gram's people, that it was almost more than I could take in. I knew I was hearing Birdella's personal opinions, yet I also felt I was hearing truths, too. I couldn't hear enough—Birdella could talk into infinity. I repeated, "How come Homer Burgess didn't like money?"

"You know!" Birdella admonished with a flick of her tiny wrist. "He was brought up so strict, and there was that thing about his father. Homer hated it when all that money came to him so easy, from the day he married Rosemary, but he could hardly have Rosemary without it. Her folks were dead by then. Those family businesses passed on to him with the marriage nearly scared the living daylights out of him. He wasn't used to it. And he always did think money was evil. That's why he did it."

"Did what?"

"Give it all away. After Rosemary died of cancer. He wasn't thinking about Selena and Ivana, I don't suppose.

His daughters were just young girls, then. Or maybe he thought going without all that luxury would turn 'em into better, hardier females."

I chewed my lip in an effort to absorb all this, make sense of it, without peppering Birdella with too many questions. But I couldn't help it, "So Selena was Ivana's sister, right? And Homer, was he not—you know, all there?"

Birdella looked sleepy as she nodded. "I think he was there."

"I meant—crazy."

"He was not crazy!" Birdella protested in raucous fury. "He wasn't, I don't know who told you that, but Homer's mind was as right as yours and mine. It was his pa who was crazy as bats. You got it mixed up. Now I'll set you straight. Homer's pa was a poor man who thought he just had to have money, see? When Homer was just a little boy, about eight, his pa was in a zinc mine accident at Joplin, Missouri. For days, the man was trapped in that dark mine, nobody to talk to. Couldn't see his own hands and feet. He went mad was what he did, went clean out of his mind."

I sucked in my breath, waiting.

"Homer's mother—oh, she was straitlaced and sickly religious, they say—insisted it was her husband's own fault. Said his lust for wealth was what brought on the tragedy. It was God punishing him. Homer's pa was babbling like a baby when they finally pulled him from the mine, and he never got any better. He lived on for years, but was more like a simple-minded young brother to Homer than the pa he needed. Homer had to take care of him. Now do you wonder why Homer hated money, the very idea of wealth? Look what it did to his father, and to him in turn. You see?"

I did, sort of, but it was the strangest story I'd ever heard.

"Homer was a very set person, he was," Birdella went on. "I always thought his mismanagement of the Halic fortune was about half-deliberate. And what he couldn't lose, he gave away. He never got over thinking money was bad. He wasn't crazy. He just had this quirk about him. A lot of us in this world got strange, funny quirks, but we aren't crazy."

I saw her point. After a while, I asked, "Can you tell me anything else?" She didn't answer. "Are you tired? Maybe you should rest now."

The old face was draggy with drowsiness as she looked up at me. "It's the hot dogs. I ate three. I always get sleepy if I eat more than one. Doctor says it's the drugs they put in wieners; he doesn't want me to eat 'em."

"I think it's chemicals, but I get the picture." I stood up and took Birdella's arm. "Would you like me to help you lie down?"

She rose slowly, nodding. "Take me to the bedroom. I'll be fine after a nap. It's the drugs in the wieners."

It was age.

The bedroom was like an oversized closet and darkened by shades drawn against the summer sunshine. The little old woman stumbled to her bed and crawled onto it. I spotted a folded afghan on the cedar chest at the foot of the bed. Old people, I knew, were usually cooler than the rest of us. I took the afghan and spread it over Birdella as she lay curled on the bed.

"May I come back later this afternoon," I whispered, "and talk to you some more when you're rested?"

Birdella nodded without opening her eyes. "I had a blue dress," she said, "periwinkle blue. If Homer had seen me in that dress, just once—" She sighed.

"You'd have knocked him out, and he'd have loved you dearly," I whispered, but she seemed to be asleep. And, I added in my thoughts, *you* might have ended up being my great-grandmother. Which wouldn't have been half bad, I thought.

I went back to Thistle Down House feeling wonderful from all that was happening to me. I spent the next few hours working on the notebook I'd started, filling in all the things Birdella Lamb had told me, making a written history. I could hardly wait to see her again, but I knew she needed rest.

Later, I went out and bought a couple of chicken breasts to cook with mushrooms, some zucchini, and salad fixings. When everything was ready, I borrowed a basket from the Gannaways and took the meal to Birdella's. We talked for another hour or two over dinner in her little kitchen. Afterward, I could hardly wait to share what I'd learned with Rom, who'd led me to Birdella in the first place. I tried several times in the evening to reach him at home, but no one answered the telephone.

Then, as I was thinking of getting ready for bed, he called me, wanting to know how my visit with Birdella had gone.

"I can't thank you enough," I told him. "Birdella is a treasure; I love her! She knew my great-grandfather, Homer. She was in love with him. And she knew my great-grandmother, Rosemary. I guess Gram's parents were rich before her father gave everything away. He had a bad experience because of money, and he just wasn't comfortable with it. Homer didn't marry Rosemary because she was rich. She was plain, but he loved her anyway. They had two kids, my grandmother, Ivana, and her sister, Selena—"

"Whoa, hold on!" Rom laughed suddenly in my ear. "I can't keep up."

"I'm sorry." I slowed down. "It's just that I'm so excited."

"I wouldn't have guessed," he teased. "Do you think you could get excited about seeing me for a while?"

Was he kidding? "I'd like to, but do you mean tonight? It's late."

"It's never too late with you. I'll meet you at the Garden Party Restaurant, and we can have a bedtime snack. How about it?"

So much for putting Rom Elliot on a back burner. "All right," I agreed.

When he arrived, pulling out a chair and moving it closer to mine, there in the nearly empty restaurant, I thanked him all over again. "Listening to Birdella Lamb I could almost see Rosemary and Homer, my great-grandparents. And Gram when she was young. And—"

Rom's good eye twinkled. "You should have heard yourself on the telephone. You sounded happy enough to take off flying, without an airplane."

"Look, I was! I am. If you've never known one thing about your family," I told him, "and then you hear these bits and pieces that are like—I don't know—they just begin to come together, and your family starts to grow— you get to know them." I shook my head and tried to swallow back the tears. I smiled as best I could.

Rom pushed my glass of milk nearer to me, motioning for me to drink. I nodded, took a few sips, and felt better. "I'm pretty sure Gamble Jones was my grandfather. I just feel it. Anyway, I want him to be. Isn't that a different name, Gamble? I would have loved to have known him in real life."

"Birdella told you about him, too?"

"Later this afternoon, yes. She brought him to life for me, talking. Her memory is fantastic for things 'way back. She said Ivana Burgess, my grandmother, was engaged to marry a well-to-do young fanner from near Rington when she met Gamble Jones." I knew I was getting starry-eyed, but I couldn't help it, recalling the true love story Birdella told me.

"Gram—*Ivana*—was nineteen at the time. She was at the home of her fiance's parents, helping to cook for a threshing crew, and Gamble was part of this nomad crew of workers. He stole her heart the moment she looked at him. Birdella says that Gamble was a handsome, happy-go-lucky drifter, incredibly romantic and great with the ladies. Ivana just forgot about her young farmer. She up and married Gamble, the drifter. Birdella said people weren't too surprised that Gamble was ready to give up his wandering ways when they saw how he was about Ivana. They were deeply in love, Rom."

I hesitated. "Should I shut up?"

He shook his head and leaned across the table to kiss my cheek. "I like to watch your face, you talk about love beautifully. Go on."

I knew I was blushing, but it didn't stop me from talking. "I understand that Gamble thought married life was just fine. Maybe because he was tired of wandering. Birdella says it was because he loved Ivana so much. They set up housekeeping in a little white cottage. It wasn't much, but there were flowers and a picket fence—like they used to write about in songs. For them it was paradise. It wasn't long before Ivana was expecting." I thought about what happened next.

"And they lived happily ever after?" Rom prodded.

I frowned. "Far from it. Gamble died a young man.

According to his gravemarker, and the records I saw, he was only twenty-two."

"My age." Rom sat back, looking somber. "So how did he die?"

"I don't know that, yet. Birdella hasn't told me. She plays out fast, talking. I'm going to see her tomorrow. I hope she can tell me something about Ivana and Gamble's baby. That person may have been my mother or father when they were grown."

For the next hour, we talked about Rom's family. His parents evidently were away much of the time, leading farm-study tours around the globe. It sounded like a fascinating way of life. The only kids in his family were himself and his sister, Anne, who had married and settled on a farm next to their parents. It was obvious Rom thought well of all of his family. Even his sister, although he admitted they had fought massively as kids. I couldn't help envying him. With effort, I thought, I might find a family of my own.

When we parted after midnight, I promised to go on a picnic with Rom on his parents' farm before going back to Oregon. I wished for more time, and again it crossed my mind, more seriously now, that I should stay longer in Kansas.

Chapter Seven

The next day I baked a batch of apple-bran muffins to take to Birdella's; we could have them with our morning tea. I was dying to hear more about Ivana and Gamble Jones, especially why he had died so young; but Birdella was too enthusiastic about the muffins, in the sunny little kitchen, to begin a serious conversation right away.

"Um-m-m!" she smacked, then licked the buttery crumbs from her fingers. She poked her small face into the sack, and her voice echoed through the crackling of paper. "I thought you might have brought jelly doughnuts, too, but I guess not."

"Next time, maybe." I smiled. "And I thought if you like, we might go to lunch one day at the Garden Party Restaurant. What do you say?"

"Eat out?" Anticipation and pleasure wreathed her face. "That'd be a treat! I'll wear a nice dress; you won't have to be ashamed of me."

"Oh, Birdella, I never would be," I protested, shocked

by her remark. "I'm looking forward to it. I think of you as my friend."

Birdella nodded, looking pleased and important. She remembered, finally, "You wanted to talk about that Gamble Jones boy, didn't you?"

"Yes. Whenever you're ready," I said loudly. Talking with Birdella was teaching me to speak clearly to everyone.

Before long, the two of us were again deep in piecing together the details of Ivana and Gamble's short life together.

"That Gamble, if he missed his life as a happy rover," Birdella remembered in a thin, crackling voice, "he didn't show it." She chuckled. "He took to husbanding like a duck to water, like he was born to it. You see"—she leaned toward me—"the story was that Gamble came from a family of fourteen children from up in Doniphan County, a little town of El wood on the Missouri River, I think it was. His pa was a poor man, a river-barge operator. Anyway, the family was near starvation most of the time."

I shook my head sympathetically and nodded for Birdella to go on.

"When Gamble turned twelve, they said, his folks decided he was old enough to make it on his own. The boy took his pa's advice and made his way to western Kansas where there was work in the wheat harvest. He hired on as a water boy, first, and then he got to be a general hand."

I broke in, "I remember you said yesterday that he was with a threshing crew when he met my grandmother."

Birdella must have forgotten. "Ivana was your grandmother?"

Although I didn't have positive proof of it yet, neither did I have evidence otherwise. And Gram had been my only family for the past eighteen years. So I answered, "Yes." I took a sip of my tea and asked, "So Gamble was a field hand for quite a few years, he was a drifter and ladies' man before he met Gr—Ivana?"

Birdella lapped almost kittenlike at her own tea before she went on. "Gamble was respectful of women, treated them nice. Men liked him 'cause he wasn't scared of hard work. You know, I always thought maybe he *wanted* a home of his own ever since he was bumped outta the family. Shoved as he was out of the nest to make his own life when he was still a child. Till he met Ivana, following the wheat and drifting was the only life he knew."

Her reasoning made sense. For a while, neither of us spoke, and then I asked the question burning in my mind, "How did Gamble die? Do you know?" My scalp crawled a little waiting for her answer, worrying and wondering.

Birdella made a face. "It was real sad. I wrote it up for all the papers; he axed his hand real bad and got blood poisoning."

I heaved a deep sigh and realized that until that moment, I'd been afraid of something much worse, like a murder. More relaxed, I asked her to tell me how it happened.

"Ivana, she wasn't home. She'd gone to see her sister, Selena, and her father, Homer, and his new family. Did I tell you . . . ? Homer, bless him. After he gave away the Halic fortune, he went back to being a mail carrier. Delivered mail about the countryside for several more years, happy as a lark. He married again, a chubby girl, widowed,

with a whole flock of children from her first husband ..."
Birdella sighed regretfully, and I thought it was because
even the second time around, Homer hadn't chosen her.

She looked at me, confused. "Where was I?"

"You were telling me how Gamble died."

"Yes. Yes, I was. Ivana was away visiting. Gamble was
sharpening an axe so he could split wood and lay the
wood by for winter. Chopped his own hand right smart.
The boy didn't care for it properly, just wrapped some old
rag around it and went right on working. There was the
harvest to finish up, too, for the man he worked for, and
he just wouldn't let up. His wounded hand got infected.
Gamble died of blood poisoning not long after, a terrible
death. He and Ivana had only been married a few
months."

It was so sad I could hardly bear to listen. "Both of
them so young," I whispered. I was beginning to see why
Gram was so sour about life—look what she'd been dealt
with from her earliest years. Her father had gotten rid of
the family's money, ending the luxury she'd been born
into and gotten used to, through no fault of her own. The
love of her life had died after such a short time with him.
Fate had been awful to her.

Birdella's next remarks substantiated my own
thoughts: "Ivana nearly went crazy with grief. Gamble
was her one true love, you see. She didn't think she could
go on without him. She blamed herself for his dying. If
she'd been home, she could have taken care of his hand,
herself. Done it right, and he'd have lived. That's what
she told herself, and me, when I questioned her for the
newspaper story. She had nightmares, bad ones, and she
never did get over it. I saw her a long time after, and she
had turned kind of hard and cold. As though she needed

a hard shell around herself to keep out any more pain. Do you know what I mean?"

I did now. Too late to try harder to penetrate that shell. I should have kept after Gram, just loved her and loved her— and melted her reserve. Gram had suffered so much even before she was out of her teens. And she was pregnant, left with a baby to care for alone after Gamble died. The child! "What about Ivana's baby?" I asked Birdella. "Yesterday you said there was a baby soon on the way after Ivana and Gamble married." *My* possible parent.

Birdella responded gravely. "Ivana was in a pickle, all right. A young widow-girl, going to have a baby. She didn't have anybody to worry about her. Her father was concerned with his new family. Her sister, Selena, married the brother of the young farmer Ivana was engaged to when she met Gamble. The young farmer didn't want her, now, but I doubt Ivana cared. She couldn't have loved him the way she loved Gamble. Alone, Ivana bore her child, a little girl. She named her for Gamble's eyes, that strange dark green-blue. Teal, it was."

"Who—wh-what—?" I tried to ask, having trouble breathing. This Teal person could be my own mother! "Tell me about the baby, please!"

"When Teal was still a baby, Ivana took work as an organist, playing music for silent movies, and even some talky ones," Birdella responded. "Ivana had to do it—she didn't have any training in anything but music. A strange, hard life. They traveled about playing at theaters in little towns all over, coming home nights when they could. I wrote them up several times in those days."

Maybe the clipping I'd found in the old suitcase had been written by Birdella, herself, back in 1924! I wanted to ask, but Birdella was on a roll with her remembrances, and I didn't want to stop her now.

"—promoter of those movies was a man named Fritz Kinney," she was saying. "A shady character, he only stayed a little bit inside the law with his doings. He kept pestering Ivana to marry him, and he finally wore her down. The marriage didn't take, of course. But I think Ivana would have stuck it out for the sake of her child, Teal. They needed food, a home, and caring for. She must have thought Fritz Kinney would provide good for them. But he abandoned them one night and stole off without a word or a trace. Ivana waited for a long time for him to come back, but I think she knew he never would."

More bad luck! I wondered if Gram had ever had another child, a son, maybe, with Mr. Kinney. If she hadn't, then I didn't see how Kinney could be my real last name. "I need to ask another question," I told Birdella. "An important one. Did Gram have any more children? Did she and Mr. Kinney have a child?"

"Oh, goodness, no. I know that for certain. Ivana and Fritz Kinney didn't have any children. There was only Teal, and Gamble was her father."

I would be willing to bet that Teal was my mother, and *that's* how I became kin to Gram, not counting the adoption. And Gram had wanted me to have her name, for reasons of her own.

I suggested taking a break to watch television when I saw that Birdella was too tired for further conversation. As I was leaving, later, I told her, "In a day or two we'll go to lunch, and I won't pester you with so many questions."

Birdella asked, "And sometime you'll take me to play bingo at the senior citizens' hall?"

I wished I could, but my time in Greendale was almost up. Then, I told her, "If there's a chance to take you to play bingo, I sure will." And I meant it. I liked Birdella a lot, and I only wished that Gram, when she was alive, had been more willing to do fun things together.

Going back to my room, I kept thinking about Gram's coolness, her dislike for an open show of feelings. When I was little and my joy got too "rambunctious" or my tears too "blubbery" Gram would exit; she'd go into her room and close the door. Usually at the moment I most needed to be hugged. If it wasn't to her room, she'd make a sudden trip to the store or the bank, leaving me alone until I had straightened out.

I could understand it more, now, but I didn't then. I was often bewildered and unhappy over the way Gram treated me. There was one time when my school had competed in a district track meet, the year I was thirteen, and I won the hundred-yard dash. Me. I hadn't been running against just kids from my school but against kids from five other schools. And I came in first. I was so proud. Forgetting everything else, I'd thrown my arms around Gram the minute I got home that day, carrying on like a crazy person, as a kid that age will. Gram had stood unmoving in my arms; I could feel her stiffness still. Then she pulled free and stalked off, her face as closed as the bank on Sunday.

My achievement dribbled to nothing; the blue ribbon in my hand seemed to lose its shine. I could only account for Gram's behavior to her dislike of vanity. She had a saying for it: "Sing small!" which meant: sober up, don't act smart-alecky. Now I wondered if Gram wasn't just dried up inside from all the bad things that had happened to her.

I hungered for affection in those days, from Gram, from a mother and father. Once, when I was about ten, I saw a young father holding the hand of his three-year-old "king" as they went door to door on Halloween night. I followed them for over an hour, hanging back, but staying close enough to sort of bask in the leftover rays of love they showed one another, the fun they were having.

I remembered Toby Doolittle from a few years later. Toby was from a very poor family, poorer even than Gram and me. On top of that, Toby was slow, he had a terrible time in school, just barely passing eighth grade. But on our graduation night, what a sight! There were two whole rows of his relatives down in the best front seats, looking so proud. And his mom clutched a bouquet of sweetpeas, flowers for a boy, the only gift she could afford. I would have traded my good report card on the spot for Toby's big night, his family.

For years I used to imagine that if I had parents, they'd be like Mrs. Doolittle and the little king's father. Before, my only ideas of what a mother and father were had come from the old black-and-white TV. Gradually, I learned that having a parent love you didn't mean getting overdosed on pizza or getting your own television or telephone. I'd seen the real thing with the little king and Toby Doolittle.

So my thoughts ran as I walked home from Birdella Lamb's.

By bedtime, I had arrived at two decisions: number one, I had to have more time here in Greendale to add to what I already had found out about myself and my family. In the morning, I would call and cancel my flight back to Oregon. I would call Penney's and tell them not to hold my job for me. My second decision was to buy a small car, something very second-hand and cheap because I didn't want to go through my money too fast. A car I could resell when it came time to go home. I was sorry now mat I'd flown to Kansas instead of driving, but I'd been scared back then of going so far. I needed a car though, to search for what I needed to know. I had to track down Teal Jones and find out if she was my mother.

I considered that the note-writer, whoever it was, might be upset when it came out that I wasn't leaving, but that couldn't be helped. I had things to do. Anyhow, Rom didn't think the note was anything to worry about, and I didn't think so, either.

A FEW DAYS LATER, I ASKED BIRDELLA IF SHE KNEW where Teal Jones might be, and if she could tell me any more about her.

Birdella sat mute for a while, then she told me, "After that man, Kinney, run out on her, Ivana got work with a farmer who raised mules, doing for the stock and working in the house as well. Then one day her child, Teal, nearly got brained by a mule's flying hoof, and Ivana quit. That's when she got a job in town with a greengrocer. I can still see that lovely little girl helpin' her mother; swatting flies away from the cabbages; stacking the apples and oranges so pretty; and skimming the foam from the top of the pickle barrels..." Her voice faded away.

"What about after that, when Teal got older, do you remember anything?"

She shook her old head. "I was gone from here a spell, although I don't think anybody paid much attention that I was gone. For quite a few years I lived in Chicago, writing feature stories for a big city paper."

"So you don't remember Teal as a teenager, or know where she might have gone from here?"

"My memory for things far back is a whole lot better than for things close in time. She might have been here when I came home to my correspondent stringin' job. I don't know." Her face took on a foggy look. "I didn't keep track of all the younger ones," she told me. "I remember Teal was a real pretty little girl. I suppose she went to high school here and then left to work. Most of the young people do that. They grow up and leave Greendale, and that's the last we hear of them."

I went back to the Cottonwood Falls courthouse and scoured the birth records again. This time I found the birth of Teal Jones, which I'd missed earlier. Teal was born in 1925. If she were still living, that meant she'd be nearly sixty now. And if Teal was my true mother, then she would have had to be about forty-one when she gave birth to me. Not common, I guessed, but not improbable, either.

I couldn't find a marriage record for a Teal Jones, but that didn't mean very much. Teal, if she did marry, could have done it anywhere, in another county, another state. There was no recorded death for Teal, either, and I was really glad about that. I meant to find her.

With more confidence than before, I now asked people about Teal. A few old-timers, merchants, could remember her, but unfortunately, none of them could tell me where she was. I would have liked to see the school records and yearbooks, for *anything* in them that might be helpful, but the school principal, Mica "Dave" Davidson still hadn't returned from California. Perhaps he meant to spend the summer there.

I ASKED ROM TO JOIN ME FOR LUNCH AT MY PLACE ONE day during my third week in Greendale. I wasn't sure before I asked that he'd accept. He had made no secret of how glad he was about my staying on in Greendale awhile, and yet in the past few days, I'd turned him down several times, when he'd asked for a date. I'd nixed another swim, a couple of movies, and on the day he'd chosen for our picnic. I'd been busy.

Now I needed him badly to talk to, but I felt guilty when he agreed to see me. Glad, but guilty. I was in a muck of depression because I'd struck a dead end, trying to find out about Teal, just when I'd been doing so well tracing Gram's family.

"I'm blocked," I complained to Rom as we ate our salads. "I found a record of Teal's birth, but that's all I can find out about her besides what Birdella told me. How could anyone be such a minus that people hardly remember her?" I wondered aloud. And then I thought to myself, look who's talking. Before now, what would anyone remember about me if they were asked? Would anyone remember that awkward little loner I used to be? Too shy to mix, always on the edge of things, but watching, play-acting in her mind that she was right in the middle? I doubted it.

Rom hadn't said anything for quite a while, and his worried look was beginning to worry me. Besides, he was cracking his knuckles. Finally, he said, "Please don't get me wrong, Bryn, because I know how you feel about finding out who your ancestors were, and all, but is it that important? I mean, the person you are at this moment, sitting over there, is what really matters." He grinned. "I like orphans. You're sweet—different. I like your mix of sophisticated beauty on the outside and simplicity and goodness on the inside. You're rare, unique. You don't need a list of ancestors, or a family history, to impress me. I'm impressed now, with you."

I couldn't believe he'd say what he'd just said. And I

couldn't believe the harshness in my own voice when I asked him, "What is this? I thought you understood?"

"I do," he implored. "But you're letting this obsession of yours blot out everything else. What about today, Bryn? Now? Us? I thought we had something, that day we spent at the lake. We could be seeing one another regularly, except you have this obsession—"

"Obsessed? Of course, I'm obsessed!" I threw down my napkin, feeling myself losing control, but his words hurt. "Why shouldn't I be, how else can I find out things?" Tears burned behind my eyes. "I knew it wasn't right to start with you, Rom. I knew it would only be trouble."

"Bryn, wait, darling, look—"

For a second it registered that he had called me "darling," that he'd said some pretty nice things about me, then my anger was back, dissolving everything else. I shoved back from the table, my face hot. "Look at things your way, isn't that what you mean? If it takes a hundred years and every hour in it, I'm going to find out who I am. If I have any family anywhere, I'm going to *know,* like you know about yourself, who gave me life in the first place. You, with your cozy family background, can't possibly know what it's like; how I feel. I only thought you did."

Rom wasn't aware that to know who you were gave you an anchor, a strength; things I was without but fighting to gain. I stood gripping the back of my chair with white knuckles, my voice strangling, "The loneliness, the root-lessness, the lack of family to care about you, what do you know about things like that, Rom Elliot?"

He argued, on his feet now, too. "A person has to make his own life, no matter what went before, and you've done a good job of that, Bryn. Yet you insist on digging up all this old junk—" He came around the table, reaching for me. "When all that really matters is you, Bryn, *you.*" He caught my arms, but I tore them away, wishing he would just leave.

It was hard to talk around the painful lump in my throat, but I snapped at him. "O-old j-junk? What I'm doing gets in the way of your having fun, isn't that the problem? Too bad, Rom—"

He caught my hand, begging. "Bryn, please—"

"No, don't touch me." I held him off, trying to control the emotion inside me. "I'm sorry I got you into this, Rom. It's my fault. I shouldn't have asked you to meet me today. We have different ideas about this relationship, and that's why it isn't working. So let's drop everything. I won't call you again; please don't call me, either." I motioned with my head to the door. I was left with a picture of Rom, his head down, walking away.

When I couldn't hear his footsteps in the hall anymore, I threw myself on the bed and cried. I felt a massive loss. What had I done?

AFTER A WHILE, I FOUND MYSELF LISTENING FOR ROM'S knock at door, but it never came. Which was best, I told myself later, washing my swollen face in the bathroom. Still, I thought, wiping away a fresh flood of tears on the towel, I had liked Rom Elliot an awful lot. More than any other human I could think of.

I hadn't wanted a friendship with Rom to get in the way of my attempts to uncover my past. But deep down, could that have partly been an excuse to cover the fact that I was unsure of myself, scared? After all, what did I know about how to carry on a serious relationship with a guy? So, maybe the real problem here was that I wasn't ready, didn't feel equipped at this point to get involved. But I shouldn't have blamed Rom. I was so mixed up.

The next day I felt no better. Smiley's grin was so accusing I almost felt like putting him in a drawer. Instead, I went to the Garden Party Restaurant and ordered an obscenity called a "Chocolate Isle." There was a tide of chocolate sauce over mountains of chocolate chip ice cream and over that clouds of whipped cream and acres of pecans. I spooned into it, deciding that if I put on ten pounds and got a jillion zits it was all right with me. At least, this wretched, gnawing pain inside me would quit.

It had been months since I'd eaten anything so utterly delicious. I relished every mouthful until the dish was empty. My stomach, though, unaccustomed to so much rich dessert, felt worse.

Fleetingly, I remembered the long, hard weeks of effort to get my body in shape. For months I'd eaten so carefully, only things that were good for me: fruit, veggies, fish and chicken mostly. I'd exercised—calisthenics for half an hour each morning and night, jogging back then, three times a week. This was Rom's fault. If I'd never met him, never been kissed by him, I wouldn't be so miserable now, wouldn't have felt the need to pig out.

He was so good-looking and nicer than any boy I'd ever been even a little bit interested in. I loved his flaws, even! His too-heavy brows, his bad habit of cracking his knuckles, his fear of flying. His stupidity at calling me "darling" at the worst possible moment. Was he too dumb to know that when you fought, you fought? *Rom*. Even in the restaurant, I couldn't stop the tears from filling my eyes. I stared at my sundae dish and knew how an alcoholic felt, drowning his sorrows in liquor. I felt drunk. I wouldn't eat chocolate again until I was eighty. Chocolate hadn't been what I wanted, anyway. I wanted Rom.

I got to my feet and weaved from the restaurant, hoping I could make it to my room before I got monumentally sick.

Chapter Eight

As I passed the Van Orden Gallery on the way to the Thistle Down, Colette saw me through the window. I didn't wonder at the alarm on her face as she motioned me to come in. I knew I must look as ghastly as I felt, and although I appreciated her concern, if that's what it was, I couldn't take more than a second. I ducked into the gallery.

Mrs. Van Orden's brow furrowed deeply. "What happened? I thought you were going back to Oregon. Your vacation—"

I shook my head. "No, I'm still here," I sputtered through clamped lips. "S-sorry I can't talk now." I fled out the door as my stomach rolled and heaved. I had to get to my room in time.

LATER, WHEN I WAS ABLE, I DIALED ROM'S HOME phone number. Maybe he had been off base a bit, making remarks about my research into my past. But one of the things I thought he had tried to tell me was that he liked me for myself, very much. Only I'd been too mad to hear it. I wanted to tell him I was wrong, too. I knew now I wanted him in my life as much as he'd shown he wanted to be in it. On the third ring, a woman's voice answered. I wondered if this was Rom's sister, or if his mother had come back from Europe. "Is Romney there?" I asked. "I'd like to speak to him. This is Bryn Kinney."

"He's not here. I'm the Elliots' housekeeper, Mrs. Lewis. Can I help you?"

"Do you know when Rom will be back, Mrs. Lewis? I'd really like to talk to him." I'd taken it for granted that I'd find Rom at home on the farm.

"He left early this morning," Mrs. Lewis told me. "He won't be back in Greendale for a week or two at least. He's gone to his school's dig up in Atchison County."

"But his eye—I thought...?"

"Oh, the doctor says his eye is fine. He got to take the patch off the day before yesterday."

The patch had come off—day before yesterday? I'd been with him yesterday. And I hadn't noticed! Too late now, I remembered a *pair* of flashing blue eyes, stormy with anger, and yes, worry, facing me across the table. I'd been too caught up in my problems to see that the patch was off. Poor guy. No wonder he was spouting off about my being obsessed; he was right.

"W-will you tell Rom, if he calls, that Bryn called him?"

"I'll tell him if I hear from him," the housekeeper promised. "But he may not be home again for weeks."

Weeks? I felt stripped of feeling as I hung up the phone. Later, in a deadened trance, I went out to the pharmacy and bought a new paperback novel to read. I wouldn't think about Rom. I'd put him totally out of my mind; it was the only way to get by. ' I read, propped up with pillows on my bed, trying to force myself to get involved with the novel's characters and their troubles. From habit, I guess, I had grabbed a romance. *Great*. I tossed the book aside and flipped on the television. The two figures floating into focus on the screen were enveloped in a tight embrace. It was everywhere! How was I supposed to forget Rom? I watched the TV show, though, and after a while, I got caught up in the plot. Later, when the story slowed, I must have fallen asleep.

A few days later I knew I had to stop telling myself that the aching, hollow feeling was from eating ice cream. I missed Rom, that's why I felt as I did. I wondered if I should head back to Oregon. My efforts to learn more about Gram, *anything* about Teal, had reached a standstill. Yet, if I stayed just a little longer in Kansas, something might turn up. Besides, Rom might call. Or he might come back to Greendale looking for me.

In the meantime, although Birdella Lamb seemed to have talked out all she knew of Gram, I continued to see her. Sometimes we sat sipping tea, talking comfortably about things we'd seen and done.

Other days, I went out in the small beat-up Celica I'd purchased from a local dealer, driving the countryside aimlessly. This was mostly cattle country, but I visited what there was to see, like the museum at Cottonwood Falls, the historic town of Council Grove located on the Santa Fe Trail, and the college at Emporia. Birdella was often able to add personal stories to what I took in.

"Have you been to Halic House yet?" she asked one time when I visited.

I perked up at the name, Halic. It was, after all, my great-grandmother Rosemary's maiden name, before she married Homer Burgess. "Halic House?" I repeated.

"What is Halic House? Where is it?" Evidently, there were some things Birdella hadn't thought to tell me.

"Rington. Halic House is over to Rington."

"But—I've heard of Rington. Isn't it close, Birdella?"

"Maybe ten miles southeast of here. It used to be one of the towns I wrote news about when I was a correspondent. Rington used to be a trading center for farmers and ranchers, and it had a lot of stores and cafes, even a livery stable. There isn't much there at all, anymore, except Halic House, a post office and store and the gas station. Just a wide spot in the road. A few homes, I suppose." Birdella scratched her nose—her mouth was turned down at the corners in vexation.

"What's wrong? Is there something about Halic House that you don't like?"

"Oh, it ain't the house. It's just that Rosemary had everything!" Birdella sighed childishly. "That beautiful mansion, and Homer—the man I wanted. I was jealous, I tell you. You know when Homer gave away the Halic money? I didn't even feel sorry; I was about half-glad it turned out like that. Of course, Rosemary was dead by then, so she didn't know it. And I should have felt sorry for the girls, Ivana and Selena. Homer wouldn't have given all that money away if Rosemary had lived; she'd have stopped him."

I thought someone should have. "Was it hard, then, for the girls, Ivana and Selena, being poor for the first time in their lives when they weren't used to it?"

"I mean to tell you! But what could they do about it? They were just young girls." Birdella shook her head. "Rosemary had provided her little ones with everything a child could want up till that time. For as long as she lived, she adored them youngsters and pampered them like little princesses. It probably worried Homer, but they had their own ponies, a nursery filled with toys, and a housemaid to serve them. Music lessons, too, although Ivana had more musical talent than Selena. Selena was pretty, but I don't recall she had any particular talents."

Not for the first time, I tried to picture Gram's blunt, arthritic fingers moving across the keys of an organ or piano. It was hopeless to imagine. What bitterness Gram must have carried, to never let on she'd been a musical person. She had never sung or even talked about music.

No, there was one time—one thing, I thought, catching my breath at the memory. Gram had been asleep on the couch, as I remembered it, maybe two years ago. And I'd been studying at the table. *The Lawrence Welk Show* had come on the TV. Gram woke up during one song, something about moonlight and roses and memories. She acted strange, as if she were somewhere else, or she didn't know where she was, or that I was there. Then, kind of crying, she suddenly turned off the television set. Worried about her, I had asked what was the matter. But Gram had snapped at me to tend to my studies, herself again—withdrawn and bitter.

I hadn't recognized it then, but Gram did have a soft side, buried very deep. She hadn't forgotten her music, not altogether, or maybe it was Gamble she was remembering.

"I'd like to hear anything you can tell me about Ivana when she was small and living at Halic House," I said aloud to Birdella, trying to shake off the sadness that had overtaken me.

"Like I said, Ivana and her sister were spoiled, but it wasn't their fault. To be fair, though, Ivana was a sweet, happy child, real fun-loving." At the description, I chewed my lip to keep from shouting something hateful against the world. To change so! Birdella went on, and not wanting to miss anything, I listened. "She was dependent on her rich mama, of course, and that's the bad part." Birdella sat back and rocked in her chair, thoughtful for some time before she went on. "Rosemary got sick when Ivana must have been— oh, twelve years old or thereabouts. Thirteen, I guess. The next two years, things began to change, after Rosemary died. That's when Homer took to giving money away. Portioning it to neighbors in need, to charities—orphans' homes, mental institutions—to any group who'd take his money."

It was an odd thing to do. I had my own ideas about money, but my philosophies hardly compared with Homer's. I liked having money. When I was growing up I had envied kids who were better off. Still, it would be wonderful to help people with money the way Homer must have. "Did he give it all away? I mean, how did the family live?" I asked Birdella.

"All of it. By 1920 the money was all gone. Ivana was about fifteen when the last of the property and their beautiful house went into somebody else's hands. Homer had gone back to being a rural mail carrier, happy as a pigeon, and no way could he afford to keep up taxes and such on a big house like that—" Birdella wiped a hand across her mouth, looking about to doze off.

"But it seems so awful," I said mostly to myself. "I mean, for Gram and her sister, for Ivana and Selena. It wasn't their fault they were born rich and got used to it. Then, to have it all suddenly yanked away. To be poor, without ever knowing before what poor is like. What a shock."

"Likely"—Birdella yawned—"but they had no choice. I doubt Homer ever fully realized the injustice he did to his young daughters. He *liked* the simple life, remember, and preferred it to any other. Maybe he thought those girls would come to feel the same way. But sometimes, I wonder...?"

Gram may have accepted being poor, I thought, but I was positive she didn't enjoy it.

This subject of money reminded me of my own small fortune. The payments had come to Gram for so many years, that Gram hadn't touched. Again, I wondered why my grandmother had never used the money. It almost had to be because she was set against the person who sent the money. But who was that?

There was still so much I had to find out. Birdella couldn't tell me everything. I smiled at her, my eyes gone misty. I was so thankful that the thought of Halic House had surfaced in her mind. I could never thank Birdella enough. She was a lamb, in more than her name!

I drove to Rington late that afternoon. What Birdella had said proved true, the town was hardly more than a wide spot in the road. The community turned out to be five miles off the main road in a grove of oak and giant elm trees. And all around for endless miles, deep prairie pastures,

I needed directions to Halic House itself, so I pulled into the dusty parking area before a combination grocery store and service station. Inside, the only sound and movement came from flies droning in lazy circles in the hot July air. I spotted a bell on the counter and struck it with my hand. A door at the back of the store opened, and a grossly overweight man wearing sagging trousers and using a cane came out, bringing with him the odor of frying ham. "Can I help you?" he asked with a wide smile. "Need gas?"

I shook my head. "No, thanks, I've got a full tank. I need directions. Can you tell me how to find Halic House?"

"Sure. The Halic House Museum is right on this same road, keep going another mile to the western edge of town. You'll see it. It's set off the road in a bunch of trees. There'll be a sign out front. You come from around here, Miss?" He puffed from the exertion of talking.

"No." I smiled. "Oregon."

"Well, we don't have a lot to show out-of-staters, but we're mighty proud of Halic House. Belongs to the community. We bought it about fifteen years ago from the folks who bought it from the original owners. It's been restored to how it used to be, and now we're creating a living craft center..."

My puzzlement must have shown on my face, because he then explained, "Out in the carriage house, the stable, and other outbuildings, we're going to have folks exhibiting horseshoeing, weaving, soap making—all kinds of stuff from the way life used to be. A living museum. But it isn't open to the public, yet. It won't be long before it's ready, though."

"I hope I get to see it," I told him. I bought a package of chewing gum and a package of unsalted sunflower seeds. "Thanks a lot."

"Sure." He turned and huffed back into the station's living quarters.

DRIVING THE LAST MILE, I TRIED TO PREPARE MYSELF. I didn't want to expect too much. It'd probably be just a huge old house holding relics from another time, no more than that. But Gram had lived in Halic House, and that alone made it special. In spite of trying to stay calm, I felt myself tensing as the big house in the grove came into view. Unconsciously, my foot left the gas pedal, and the car slowed to a near stop. Quickly, I looked into the rearview mirror, but no one was behind me.

The mansion, and truly it was a mansion, I saw, rose grandly, four stories of alcoves, windows, and turrets, all trimmed beautifully with gingerbread. My throat dried as I took it all in, awestruck. The house sat on a small rise, with huge trees beyond the outbuildings. Among the smaller outbuildings, workers were sawing and painting.

My chin began to tremble, and I bit my lip to keep from crying. Gram, my own *Gram,* had lived here? Somehow, hardly aware of what I was doing, I got the car turned into the drive. I braked and turned off the motor, then continued to gawk, my knees feeling watery as I got out of the car.

How could it be true? Gram—raggedy, work-worn, close-mouthed Gram—had come from this? Birdella wouldn't lie. But what a comedown for my grandmother, far more than I had guessed.

I took the brick walk and steps up to the columned side porch, which was wrapped around the front third of the house. Coming up the drive, I noticed other porches and entries, but I thought this must be the main one. I opened the door and a cheery-faced little man rose from behind a polished desk. The dimly lit foyer was comfortably cool, and I sighed, relishing it after the heat of the outdoors.

"Welcome!" the curator said. "Would you like to sign our guest book, Miss?" He pointed to a register that lay open, with an elegant pen in a holder alongside.

I nodded, returning his friendly smile. As I signed, I saw that there had only been about a half-dozen or so guests before me today. That would no doubt change when the craft center opened.

"Would you like me to guide you through the museum? It's no extra charge," the old curator offered.

"Thanks ..." I turned him down with a smile. "... but I'd like to walk through by myself if you don't mind." I gave him the three-dollar admission charge and took a deep breath, my chin lifted. I had never experienced anything like what I would be going through in the next hour or so. I wanted the experience to be totally mine, without distraction. It would be like walking through a time warp into Gram's childhood. A Gram I hadn't really known at all before this summer.

I followed a crimson velvet rope to the doorway of the first room, a sitting room according to a sign by the door describing it. The room was furnished in rich dark woods, olive velvet furniture, and oriental carpets. The sight of a mannequin near a library table in the corner startled me. The figure, dressed in a dark blue turn-of-the-century gown trimmed in white, seemed almost alive. The name "Rosemary" flew into my mind.

Shaking, I continued on, scolding myself for being dumb. I'd have to be careful not to get carried away.

The color red predominated in the music room. When I caught sight of the ornate piano near the alcove window, I shook my head and fought not to cry. Gram as a child must have taken lessons at that very piano. Through a film, I pictured a small girl with bows in her long curls, wearing a ruffly dress, fingers bouncing and gliding across the keys. I closed my eyes and swallowed hard.

From room to room I walked, transfixed, my whole being caught in a tide of emotion such as I had never felt before.

Although most of the rooms were small, they were lavishly furnished. Most had stained glass windows, each had a fireplace of delicate blue and pink translucent onyx stone and a chandelier of white alabaster or crystal. Such riches, such elegance. But Homer Burgess hadn't wanted it; he thought it was the devil's work. It made me mad enough to hit something, remembering Gram's life when she had next to nothing.

My own memories began at about age three. Gram had brought me from someplace still unknown to me, to settle in a remote logging town in the Northwest, I thought around the year 1969. "Home" those first years in Oregon was an abandoned, false-fronted store at the far end of Main Street. Rent was no doubt very low; I remembered that old drapes covered the store's windows to make it private, our home.

Comparing that barren, chilly old store with this palace brought a sour taste of anger to my throat. Poor, poor Gram. She had taken whatever jobs came her way, over the years, I recalled. Such a struggle, cooking for loggers, taking in sewing. In the summers we went down to the valley to pick fruit or vegetables for pay. Evidently, whatever pride Gram had been born with had crumbled long before she came to Oregon. Remembering our summers though made me feel a trifle better.

I've always liked summer the best. We were around people more, then, although I hadn't actually mixed very much with them. Gram wouldn't permit it. Anyway, stooped over a big bean bucket, yanking beans off the vines and dropping them in, I could listen to the conversations going on up and down the other bean rows. About life in other places. Funny happenings that would make me smile to myself, listening. And—the singing. Pickers seemed to be great ones for making their own music, singing lustily, ballad after ballad, and someone would have a guitar. Surely, listening to the music, Gram had felt lighter, too? Happier. Even if she couldn't say it, she must have.

For years I'd been aware that others around us considered Gram strange, hostile, a bit crazy, maybe. I'd pretty much turned a deaf ear, paid no attention, choosing to defend her in my mind because she was my person, my grandmother. Anyway, in a life mostly bleak, those summers were sunshine and song in lots of ways.

I STROLLED ON THROUGH THE MANSION. IN THE library, I caught up with other sightseers, a couple. Farmers, I thought, probably on vacation. The wife was exclaiming over a gold-framed painting of a clipper ship that hung on the wall. I left them standing there and went on alone past an awesome dining room and several bedrooms.

But I began to shake violently when I reached the nursery. It wasn't a large room, and the two canopied beds, tiny tables and chairs, and shelves of toy dishes and dolls made it seem even smaller. It was the mannequin of a child in the center of the room, a child about five years old, poised at the handle of a doll carriage, that held my gaze and made my heart turn over. *Gram*. The small Ivana.

My throat seemed to close, and at the same time, sobs rumbled up from deep within. I clamped my lips tight and whimpered. Then I was turning, shivering, trembling, running from the nursery, down the long carpeted halls, frantic to find the front door. At last, I reached the foyer, running past the gaping old curator at his desk, hurtling by a tall gentleman who'd just entered. I stumbled and almost fell down the steps, then I was opening the car door. Once behind the wheel, my fumbling hand tried to turn the key in the ignition, without success. But I had to get away.

Gram was dead, and there was so much I hadn't known about her. So much I still didn't know about myself. But finding out was hurting. I got the car running and turned back toward Greendale. If only Rom would be there—to comfort me, make this pain for Gram go away. But he wouldn't be there.

Chapter Nine

I had been in my room for about fifteen minutes when my phone rang and Mrs. Van Orden asked me to meet her downstairs. I was in the process of changing into a cool top and shorts, so I told her it might be a few minutes.

Later, coming down the stairs, I saw Colette waiting near the front door. Her face was set, her behavior stiff. Something must be wrong, I thought, but I couldn't figure out how it could involve me. "Mrs. Van Orden?" I approached her. "Should we sit down? Would you like to come up to my room?"

Colette turned. "No, that won't be necessary. This will only take a few minutes. But I wanted to tell you in person." Perspiration beaded her upper lip, a contrast to the coldness in her eyes and voice. *Toward me?*

"What's the matter?" She was scaring me, and I didn't like it.

"Your car! I saw you park it today, so I know the awful thing is yours. The green Celica. This is three times you've parked it almost directly in front of my store and left it to come here. Where do you think my customers park? I realize this place doesn't have its own parking lot, but I must tell you, *do not park in front of my store."*

I couldn't have been more surprised. Another thing, I must have been spoiling for a fight. This had been a particularly upsetting day. For whatever reason, I didn't fall apart under Colette's sudden unfriendliness, as I might have once. Instead, I held my ground and matched her look, "Oh?"

"Don't act smart with me, young lady. I'm serious. I can't imagine what you need a car for anyway. Since you're only going to be in Greendale a short time, it's hardly necessary. There are cars enough blocking the streets."

I couldn't believe this. It wasn't her business, but I answered, "I've changed my plans. I'm staying in Greendale indefinitely."

I was further startled by the look of fear my announcement brought to her face. Colette slumped and the long polished nails of one hand stabbed at the palm of the other. Her mouth worked nervously, "Wh-what d-do you mean?"

"I'm in Greendale to find out about my family," I told her, not feeling quite so angry myself, now. "I'm not finished, and I can't leave till I am."

Colette straightened, and her face took on a closed look. She said in a flat voice, "Just remember about the car. I don't want you to ruin my business, too." She gave me her back and stalked out the front door.

I stood there thoroughly confused. *Too?* What did she mean by that? I was unable to believe that such an idiotic scene could have taken place. What on earth had gotten into her?

I couldn't imagine anyone being so upset over a car

parked in the wrong place, but I'd move it. I doubted that was the real problem, though, and my earlier vague suspicions that Mrs. Van Orden might have written the note jelled. The woman didn't want *me* here in Greendale; it wasn't my car, but me. I shivered. Colette had acted as if my very presence was poison.

Colette Van Orden had written the note pressing me to get out of town, I was certain now. But I hardly knew what to do about it. I only knew I couldn't leave, yet. For a flash, I considered facing her down and demanding to be told what she knew, why she didn't want me here. But I realized she would probably stick with her story about my car being parked in the wrong place. So I would just wait. *Whatever* Colette had against me, and whatever she meant to do about it, I'd deal with when the time came. In the days that followed, I found a new parking spot, and I avoided the woman in general, going nowhere near her gallery.

It took nerve to return to Halic House after my hasty exit, but I knew I had to do it. For one thing, I wanted to see what I'd missed. I wanted to see everything all over again and take pictures. In the photograph album I had bought my first week here, I had put the developed shots I'd taken of Greendale, scenes at the cemetery with Gamble's grave, and many of the surrounding countryside. Now, I could add shots of Halic House, inside and out.

The elderly curator looked apprehensive when I appeared at Halic House a few days later. To put him at ease right away, I decided to tell him the truth. "I'm sorry for running out of here like a crazy person the other day. I didn't mean to worry you. You see, sixty-one years ago, my Gram—" I broke off and tried, again. "I was raised by my grandmother. As a little girl, she lived in this house. The mannequin in the nursery—I don't know—somehow it made me think of her, and it upset me. I didn't mean to create a scene."

The old man listened. "Who are you, Miss?"

I smiled at him, wishing I could give him the complete truth, but I couldn't when I didn't know myself. "My name is Bryn—Kinney. My grandmother was Ivana Kinney, but she was born a Burgess. Her mother was Rosemary Halic Burgess."

He stared at me open-mouthed, then he reached for my hand and shook it. "The missing sister. Ivana is the missing sister. You're her granddaughter?"

I nodded. Until proven otherwise, I was.

"I'm Mr. Thomas Snow, and I've managed the Halic House Museum from the beginning." His face was infused with eagerness now, as he gripped my hand, continuing to shake it. Finally, he let go and he came around the desk. "Can you tell us about Ivana, where she's living now? This new information should be included in the history of Halic House."

"She's dead," I had to tell him. "For the past fifteen years she—we—lived in the Northwest. Oregon, to be exact. But Gram died this past spring."

"Oh, I'm sorry to hear it." He looked up. "No one knew where Ivana'd gone. She disappeared without a trace. Not even her sister, Selena, knew where she went or why. It was thought that Ivana might be dead. Such a pity. Well, now we know."

"What about Selena, Gram's sister? Is she living? Where is she?"

"Gone, too," he shook his head. "A widow, she passed

away two years ago. The last of the Halics, those two sisters. Now, all the older ones are gone."

"Gram had a daughter, Teal Jones. Have you heard of her?" I asked, my throat feeling dry.

He shook his head. "We knew Ivana married twice and there was a daughter by the first marriage. When we wrote up the history of Halic House, we tried to locate this daughter for more information, but we weren't successful. She, too, had simply disappeared. Not that that is unusual. A lot of people live here for a time and then move away, and nobody keeps track of where they've gone."

"You mentioned a history of Halic House; could I see it?"

"Of course. It's a little printed pamphlet we put together for tourists. We sell it for one dollar." He rummaged in a desk drawer. "We're almost out of copies. When we reprint, we'll use whatever information you can give us about your grandmother, Ivana." In a moment he handed me a small orange pamphlet. "Here we are. Found one." He shook his head when I started to open my purse. "Oh, my, no, it's yours. Please keep it. We're just happy you've turned up."

I took a chair on the opposite side of the foyer, anxious to scan the pamphlet. It was brief, telling how the first Halics, my great-great-grandparents had come to this part of Kansas following the Civil War. They'd come from Indiana, where they had raised fine horses. That Halic family had consisted then of George and Mary Halic and their daughter, Rosemary. George was an ambitious man, who rather quickly built a small empire on the Kansas soil he'd bought. He made a fortune in raising wheat and cattle, and right after the turn of the century, oil was found on land he owned in the central part of the state.

I read on for a few minutes, and then I leaned my head back in the chair and closed my eyes. The rest of the pamphlet revealed nothing I didn't already know from Birdella. For instance, Rosemary was a great horse-woman, and she had married a mail carrier named Homer Burgess, who, unwisely or not, had gotten rid of the fortune George Halic had worked so hard to build.

And Rosemary and Homer had had two daughters: Ivana who was very merry and musically talented; and pretty Selena who— My eyes flew open. I sat up and flipped quickly through the pamphlet once more. I found what I'd only skimmed over a while ago. *Selena's descendants*. Selena, I read now, had married a farmer named Gabriel Bassett. The Bassetts had a son and daughter, Giles and Grace. Who were possibly living!

I tucked the pamphlet in the outer pocket of my handbag and took up my camera. Standing, I asked Thomas Snow, "May I take pictures?"

"Please do. After all, the mansion and everything in it once belonged to your family."

I thanked him, and then I said, "One more thing. You said Selena is no longer living. But the pamphlet mentions her children, Giles and Grace. Do you know anything about them? Are they living and did they stay in these parts? I'd like to talk with them."

He nodded, obviously pleased to be of help. "Giles moved to California. He has orange groves there. But Grace married a Fontaine boy, and they now live at Great Bend."

"Great Bend, Kansas?"

"Yes." He looked thoughtful, smiling. "Of course, Grace and Jim Fontaine are not kiddies, the way I remember them most of the time. They're grandparents by now. You're going to see them? You'll like Jim and Grace. They're farmers. Good family. They come to visit Halic House whenever they're by this way."

"I do want to see them, but do you have an address?"

"Yes, yes. When were they here last? In March, I think." He thumbed back through the guest register to March, then April, running his bony finger down the page. "Here they are." He pointed and handed the open guest book to me.

I took it, looked at the address, and copied it into my notebook. "I can't thank you enough," I told Mr. Snow. "You've been a wonderful help."

"My pleasure, my pleasure. It's a delight to meet a descendant of the Halics."

I nodded, smiling, and turned to begin my second tour of Gram's childhood home.

IT WAS LESS THAN A HUNDRED MILES TO GREAT BEND, but it was the longest distance I had ever driven alone. Once I had crossed the Cottonwood River, however, Highway Fifty-Six was paved road all the way. I enjoyed seeing the towns I passed through—Marion, McPherson, Lyons—here in the heart of Kansas, in the heart of summer.

Only as I neared Great Bend did my tension mount, not being sure just how the Fontaines would receive me. Situated on a curving sweep of the Arkansas River, the town was much larger than Greendale. With some floundering, I drove around slowly until I located a cafe where I parked the car in a side parking lot. The day was sweltering. Heaving a sigh, I went into the cafe and ordered a large Pepsi, taking my time with it.

I could hardly believe how nervous I felt. The Pepsi gone, I freshened up in the restroom. Then finally, having run out of things to postpone the eventual meeting, I set my shoulders and made my way to the pay phone in the corner of the cafe. I found the Fontaines' number, dialed it, and with a phony calmness I told the woman who answered who I was and why I was calling.

There was a predictable silence. I realized too late that I should have called or written from Greendale before coming all the way here. Then the woman was speaking again, and I could hardly believe my ears. "I'm Grace Fontaine, honey, your first cousin once removed! Please hurry to the farm as fast as you can get here, I'm dying to meet you!" The same kind, warm voice went on to give me directions to the farm. I scribbled quickly, elated, the phone cradled to my ear by my shoulder.

A very short time later, I drove up a paved drive to a large, sprawling ranch-style home, very modern; white with red brick trim. The colorful flowerbeds of petunias and other flowers that edged the spacious lawn bloomed gloriously in the sun, matching my rising spirits. Beyond the house was an enormous red barn and other tidy outbuildings, an honest-to-goodness modern farm, my first to actually visit. Already I was more than glad I'd come!

Still, I needed several deep breaths before I got out of the car. At the front door, I reached for the doorbell, but before I could touch it, the door flew open. A woman, perhaps in her mid-fifties, or older, stood beaming at me. From the fashionable cut of her short graying blond hair to her figure, trim in white shorts and blue top, Grace Fontaine didn't fit my previous ideas of a farm wife. Her lovely skin wasn't by any means "etched deep by wind and sun," although she had laugh lines around her soft green eyes. There was no "ample bosom covered by a cotton print apron" either. Rather, Grace looked as if she might have invented aerobic dance.

"Hi," I said nervously. "I hope I'm not butting in—?"

Grace answered by catching my hand and pulling me into a hug. "Nothing of the kind," she said with a soft, gentle laugh. "Kin is always welcome at the Fontaine Farms. Come in, darling. Let's get you comfortable. Please excuse how hot this damn house is. I've been canning today, and the air-conditioner is on the fritz. The air-conditioner likes to quit on the hottest days of the year." She laughed.

"It's really all right. I'm starting to get used to the heat here. Oregon is so cool a lot of the time."

"Does it rain out there as much as they say it does?" Her eyes twinkled as she waved me to a white overstuffed couch in the living room.

"Easily." I grinned, then I spoke more seriously. "There's something I need to make clear from the start. I don't have positive proof that I am your kin, although I think I am. That's why I'm here, to learn what I can about my past. The only thing I know for sure is that I was raised by Ivana Kinney, who was a Halic descendant, and I always understood she was my grandmother."

Grace sat with her arm folded and her chin in her hand. She looked puzzled. "I don't get it. Why would you have any doubts that Mama's sister, Ivana, was your real grandmother?"

"It's a long story," I admitted, shrugging, "but I'll keep it short. The only legal document I have is a delayed birth certificate Gram got at the time she became my legal guardian. My real parents aren't listed on it, only my birthdate and the place where I was born, Greendale. Gram would never tell me anything about who my parents might have been. She was a very close-mouthed person. Her past, and mine, have been pretty much a blank book until this summer. Because she would never say, I don't know who she got me from, or why. I'm pretty sure she was my true grandmother, but it's mostly a feeling. I have no proof." I added, "But I don't have any real reason to think otherwise, either."

Across from me, Grace sighed. "God, not to know who—" She shook her head. "I saw Aunt Ivana a few times when I was little, but not a lot. She and Mama sort of went their separate ways after they grew up and married. Mama, Selena to you, married—how shall we say?...well. And after Aunt Ivana turned down my Uncle Claude, my father's brother, in marriage, she seemed to suffer one piece of bad luck after another."

"That's true," I agreed, "but it wasn't all bad for Gram. I'm told she was very happy with Gamble Jones, her first husband. Of course, he died soon after they got married. But she did have that one true love for a while."

"So I've heard," Grace said with a smile. "Mama always said Gamble was such a sweetheart, and it was no wonder her sis married him. Uncle Claude was a stuffed shirt." She laughed merrily, then went on more seriously, "And you know, Bryn, I've been watching you, and I'm convinced Ivana was your real grandmother. It may not be proof enough for you, but you look like family. You have several familiar features that I've seen in pictures of even the oldies. Your turned-up nose, the shape of your brow, and big gray-green eyes have run in the family for generations. But your chin is what really strikes me. You have that little dimple, not an actual cleft, just like your Grandfather Gamble had."

"D-do you mean it, really?" My heart pounded madly in my chest. I felt a smile spread across my face. "I've never seen a picture of Gamble Jones. And Gram never mentioned him." It was so little to go on, though, family likeness, when you thought about it. I shouldn't bank on being Gamble Jones's granddaughter for sure. Not yet. Less excited, I said, "If your mother, Selena, and Gram weren't on good terms, then you probably don't have any pictures of them—Ivana and Gamble?"

"On the contrary. I have Mama's photo albums, and there are pictures of the two girls when they were growing up at Halic House, and lots of others. Have you seen Halic House?"

I nodded. "It's wonderful. And it's going to be even better when the Pioneer Craft Center is ready for the public." When I knew Grace better I might tell her of my first traumatic visit there, when the mannequins seemed alive.

Grace said, "It's a beautiful place, too bad it was lost to the family. Dear old Grandpa Homer, he surely did his number." She laughed easily at many things, I was finding out, a delightful laugh that tickled a person and made them laugh, too. "Well, that's how the cookie crumbles," she said. "At least, the mansion is still standing, and it's a nice place the family can visit."

Grace suggested that we save the photograph albums until after dinner. As her guest, I couldn't argue, but I was dying to see them. Anticipation made it hard for me to pay attention as Grace talked, moving about her kitchen preparing the meal—while I sat on a stool, waiting less than patiently. But I gathered that Grace's husband, Jim, was out of town. And we would be joined at dinner by their youngest son, Ted, the only one living at home. With his brothers, Ted managed the farms. Grace and Jim were all but retired, having turned over most of the farming to the younger generation.

Just when Grace began to grumble that dinner would be ruined, her tardy son Ted plunged through the back door into the kitchen. He slid to a halt when he saw me on the stool. "Whoa," he said softly. "Whoa." He took a couple of steps backward and surveyed me, his sun-browned hands resting on his lean hips. "Ma, what've you brung me?" he asked.

I couldn't help laughing as I looked back at Ted Fontaine. He was deeply bronzed, blond, medium tall, and lean. Mischievousness twinkled in his eyes.

"Son, I want you to meet Bryn Kinney, your second cousin," Grace introduced us. "This is Ted, honey."

"A girl with your looks shouldn't be related to me at all," he drawled. He looked at his mother. "First cousins aren't supposed to marry, but we can, can't we, Ma?"

"You scamp, behave," his mother ordered with a warm smile. She told me, "There are already so many girls hooked on him it's a disgrace."

"I can believe it," I said softly. Ted was quite a hunk, but not any match, of course, for Rom Elliot. Still, it might be fun to have a gorgeous male cousin.

DINNER WAS DELICIOUS. BUT I HAD TO PROTEST WHEN Ted tried to get me to take seconds on everything. "I can't, really. Even though your mom is a fantastic cook, and everything they say about home-grown farm food is true, I can't eat another bite."

"Not even Ma's gooseberry pie? It's Grandma Fontaine's recipe."

"I'm sorry." I shook my head and smiled.

While Grace and Ted were eating their pie, I decided to bring up the subject of Gram's daughter, Teal Jones, who would be Grace's first cousin. She was maybe my mother, and I wanted to know everything about her.

"Oh, yes." Grace looked across at me. Her eyebrows rose, and she looked puzzled as she considered. "I knew my cousin, Teal, but we were never close. I always wished we'd been better friends. But we didn't see a lot of each other, and when we did—" She sighed. "To tell you the truth, we didn't have much in common. Teal was— different. Even when she was so little you wouldn't think she'd notice, she was terribly dissatisfied with their—with Ivana's—situation; the way they lived. And Ivana was too proud to take help from Mama."

I could understand all of it; I had memories of my own.

"Teal," Grace went on, "seemed to be made of strong stuff, really strong, you know what I mean? The sort of person who toughens, rather than weakens, from adversity. I think her mother went the opposite way," she added with an apologetic grin. "But Teal had goals she meant to attain, even when we were kids. High goals. She was reading all the time, as I remember, dreaming and planning. I guess that's what made her seem so out of step with the rest of us. We were only interested in things like playing jacks and seeing the next Saturday matinee." Her nose wrinkled in a wry grin.

"What did she look like?" I wanted to hear more, much more.

"Beautiful. Teal was beautiful. Even though they didn't have much money, she was always clean, neat, and as well turned-out as possible. She had black hair and eyes the strangest blue, well, *teal,* that's the color. I didn't realize it till now, but I guess that's how she was named. Anyway, going beyond her looks, Teal had a manner that —that kind of pulled away from you, you know? A haughtiness. Or maybe she was shy, it's hard to say, now. She wasn't easy to know."

I was thinking as Grace talked that there were things about Teal that reminded me of myself. The shyness and trying hard to look nice. I asked quietly, "Do you know where Teal is now?"

Grace looked stumped. "Gosh, I don't know. I don't think I've seen her since we were beginning high school. I don't have to tell you that that was a long time ago. I'm sure she moved as far away from Greendale as possible, though. As I said, we were never close. We didn't keep in touch. A pity, I can see that now."

"I think she's my mother," I spoke into the silence that followed.

"Teal!" Grace was astounded. "Teal had a child? Of course, if it turns out that Ivana was your real grandmother, then Teal would have to be your mother." She sat back. "God, not to know for sure who your real mother is! It's crazy. Honey, how can you handle it?" She looked close to tears herself.

"N-not very w-well," I answered truthfully, my own smile shaky. "That's why I'm doing all this digging."

"Your grandmother must have been a world champion clam," Grace raged, "not to tell you one thing about your parents. How could anyone be that secretive? Good Lord!" She began to gather silverware in agitation, clanging it into an empty platter. "Honey"—she shook a fork—"I want you to know that we're behind you in this. If there's anything we can do to help, yell. And you're to consider us your family, hear? You remember we're here for you from now till doomsday, *your family*."

Ted, who had remained silent through all this, now agreed with his mother. "You bet!"

I was so grateful to them I could have cried. As it

was, I couldn't speak. Fortunately, Grace wasn't quite finished, anyway. "Another thing," she said, "I want you to come to our family reunion. It's the Fontaine reunion, not a Halic-Burgess sort, but you never can tell who'll show up. There might be somebody there who can tell you about Teal, or about yourself, even. People born and raised around Rington, Mumford, and Greendale come from every corner of the country for the reunion."

It sounded like the perfect idea. I nodded my head and managed to ask, "When is it?"

"The second week in August; it's always the second week in August. It'll be held at a park that's between Rington and Mumford. You definitely have to be there, honey."

"I will be." That was a little more than two weeks away, but I'd already decided to stay on in Kansas as long as it took to find out what I needed. Maybe, though, I should think about finding a part-time job. I had money, but it wouldn't last forever. And there was my future to think about.

"With you at the reunion, it won't be such a drag." Ted broke into my planning. "Now, how about going to a movie with me tonight?"

"Nothing doing, you devil," his mother said. "Bryn and I have a date with a stack of photo albums in the living room. Now scat on out of here and get yourself another girl."

Ted looked reluctant, but he shrugged helplessly. I smiled at him and gave him a tiny wave.

Chapter Ten

I sat next to Grace on the sofa, a photo album spread across our laps. There were not a lot of pictures of importance to me among those of the Bassetts, Fontaines, and their friends. But each time Grace pointed to a photo, saying, "There," my heart leaped and I drank the picture in.

There were quite a few of Halic House in the early days. Scenes of the house with snow piled high in front, a man and woman and two fur-bundled little girls waving from a horse-drawn sleigh. There were springtime pictures of the little girls having tea parties and birthday parties in the garden. Several showed Rosemary Halic Burgess seated on a magnificent horse, herds of cattle and horses in the background.

Homer, a dough-faced little man with a small mustache (what special thing Birdella saw in him, I couldn't tell), was in some of the horse pictures with Rosemary, invariably looking about to fall off his mount. I had to hold back giggles at his pictures. Rosemary's whole life must have been hard for him to adapt to.

"This can't be Gram," I finally spoke aloud. But the photo was labeled, *Ivana Burgess, dressed for her recital.* The girl in the picture was about thirteen. Her dark wavy hair was bobbed short, her cheeks looked dark with color and they were high and rounded in a smile. She stood with her hands low in front, thumbs wrapped one around the other and her forefingers touching. Her dress was of a dark, silky material, trimmed with something feathery at the scoop neck, sleeves, and around the tiered skirt. Vaguely, she looked like Gram. And yet, so different. Gram very young and happy. Rich and well cared for. The picture must have been taken before Gram's mother, Rosemary, got sick, I was thinking.

"Here's Ivana again, with Gamble, her husband, right after they married."

The picture was tiny. Even so, I could see that the couple cared for each other. Ivana sat on a rock wall, her legs crossed at the ankles, her arm through Gamble's as he stood on the ground leaning against her. They looked so happy, so *young.* Gram was right to choose Gamble, I had no doubts. I sighed. "I wish there was a better picture of Gamble Jones. I'd like to see his chin close up."

"There is another one. Just him." Grace took the album and flipped through it. "Here." It was a large picture of a young man in his early twenties.

I saw the dimple in his chin, first. My hand shook as I covered the top half of Gamble Jones's face, leaving only his mouth, chin, and jaw. I might have been looking at a picture of myself! I stuck my tongue tight against the inside of my cheek as I fought to hold back the tears that burned in my eyes. I looked at Grace.

"Good Lord, what a resemblance!" She looked at me, then at the picture, and back at me again. "I'll settle for that proof, right there. Kid, you're the spitting image of your Grandpa Jones. Not just his chin, his mouth is yours, too."

I wasn't able to answer. The picture wasn't proof, of course, but I did feel better. Because I did look like him. I had already liked Gamble Jones, from what I'd heard about him. Studying his picture, he captured my heart totally. His head was tipped in the photograph ever so slightly; one eyebrow rose higher than the other in an easy-going, devil-may-care expression. It was the twinkle in his eye that caught me. And that's where his smile mostly was, I saw, in his eyes rather than on his mouth. The look was for Gram, I guessed, for the young Ivana. His hair was combed back in shiny waves, a small ringlet falling handsomely onto his forehead.

Looking at him, my heart nearly broke. *Why did you have to die so young?* I asked the picture silently. *You never got to be my grandpa, really. But if you had, I know we'd have gotten along; we'd have had wonderful times and I would have loved you so much. It's good you didn't know what your dying did to Gram, how she became, after. I'm sorry your dreams and hers never had a chance to come true. It wasn't fair. But I promise you this, if it turns out you were my grandfather, and I'm sure you were, my children and my children's children will know about you. They'll love your memory as much as I do, as much as I would have loved you if you'd had a chance to grow old and know me.*

When Grace saw the tears running down my face, she made a soft clucking sound. Gently, she took the album from me, and with care, she removed the photo of Gamble Jones from the album and placed it in her lap. She turned the pages and systematically removed the photographs of Gram when she was young at the recital. Gram and Gamble together right after they married, and others of Homer and Rosemary, stuffing them into my hands.

There was only one picture of Teal. Taken from a distance, it showed a child of about five years—a forlorn little figure looking lost next to the trunk of a big tree, her hair blowing against her cheek, the sun obviously in her eyes. "I don't know what to say," I sobbed.

"It's my pleasure, honey," Grace said firmly. "And these pictures are rightfully yours, anyway. I don't need any proof of who you are."

WE HAD LOST TRACK OF TIME. I REMEMBERED VAGUELY, later, that Ted had come home from the movie sometime and had told us goodnight. Because the hour was late, Grace insisted that I spend the night, and I agreed. As it turned out, I didn't go back to Greendale the next day, nor the next. I stayed and toured the farm with Ted as my guide. The second evening, I went to a movie with him. The afternoons Grace and I spent sightseeing and shopping. I had never felt more welcome anywhere. My newly found cousins made me promise to attend their upcoming reunion and begged me to come back and see them before that if I could.

I RETURNED TO GREENDALE FEELING MORE SETTLED and happy than I had felt in a long while. Then, at the Thistle Down, I spotted a letter addressed to me on the hall table. I felt a cold dread, wondering if Colette was issuing a real threat, this time. But it was from Rom!

I was home for a weekend visit. Hoped to see you. Mrs. Gannaway said you were out of town. Maybe we can get

*together another time. I want to apologize for the fuss we had. It
was my fault. Okay? I care.*

Love, Rom

I was so disappointed at missing Rom that I almost
wished it had been a note from Mrs. Van Orden. I had a
strong urge to go looking for him. Except that I'd never
been one of those girls who chased after guys. And more
and more I was thinking I had to find at least a part-time
job to cover some of my expenses. Best to turn my attention to that, I decided. It wasn't what I wanted to do,
though. Rom just had to come home again, soon. He
cared about me; I had the note to prove it.

THE GREENDALE BULLETIN, WHEN I SCANNED THE
help-wanted ads a few minutes later in my room, offered
little. The Thriftway Cleanery needed a shirt-presser, but
that hot, back-room job sounded dull, dull, dull. I
couldn't feel any more enthusiastic about the few waitress jobs listed. Then I noticed a boxed ad off to the side
that I hadn't seen before; it was advertising for a female
guide for the new Halic House Pioneer Craft Center.

If I could get that job it would be perfect, I decided,
better than perfect. What fun to show off the house
where Gram grew up. But I'd have to get over being
emotional about it, provided I got the job. The notice
advised prospects to contact Mr. Thomas Snow, Curator,
for further information. I was glad we'd already met and
talked. That would make it easier. I could hardly wait to
see him, but first I needed to wash off some road dust
and put on a neat skirt and blouse. The more I thought
about it, the more I wanted the job.

Within the hour, I was in the car again, driving to

Halic House. There, I cornered Mr. Snow and expressed my desire to apply for the guide job.

"You know," he beamed, shaking a finger, "I was hoping you would see our ad and be interested in the position! As a Halic descendant, you're the perfect person to act as a guide and hostess of our new Halic Pioneer Craft Center for children. Of course, it will be part-time; we plan to keep it open just three days a week at the start."

"That would be fine." Part-time work was what I wanted, since I still needed to continue my search. "Please tell me more about it. I've seen some of the work going on, the painting and fixing up. But what would I have to do, exactly?"

"Of course, you need to know that," he acknowledged. "You see, the carriage house here, and the stable and outbuildings were just standing idle, and it seemed such a waste. Then, the members of the County Heritage Association got the idea of establishing the pioneer craft center. To enable youngsters, chiefly, to learn what life was like a hundred years ago. In the outbuildings, craftspeople will demonstrate blacksmithing, wool carding, weaving, butter churning, and so on. Children will be encouraged to touch and try quilting, candle-making, carding, and they will make apple and corn husk dolls as well."

I listened carefully as Mr. Snow went on. "Your job will be to welcome the children as they arrive, and then guide them along from craft to craft, explaining the process and engaging their interest in it. Not a difficult job. And we'd like for you to wear an old-fashioned calico dress. As I said, we want to do what we can to bring history alive for our visitors. You, as a Halic descendant, would help so much to further that aim."

"I'm sure I can do it, and I'd love it!" I told him. "Has anyone else applied?"

"A few local girls. I must admit, you would be my first choice. But it will be up to the County Heritage Association to decide. The decision will be made at the end of the week when we've had a chance to consider all of the applicants."

Even if it turned out that I wasn't a true Halic descendant, which I doubted more than ever would happen, I was probably closer to being one than anyone else in town, having been brought up by Gram. Mr. Snow brought me the application forms, and I filled them out carefully and happily.

I had several days to wait for the outcome. I filled them by taking Birdella to lunch again, and I took her also for a long ride in the country. On another day, I returned with tools to the cemetery for several hours' work on Gamble Jones's grave, finishing with a bouquet of fresh flowers. I wrote long notes about my newest findings from my visit to the Fontaines, and I brought my album up to date with the photos that Grace had given me.

Having made the decision to stay in Greendale, I made a telephone call to my banker in Salem and asked him to transfer my account to the Greendale bank. I wrote a note to my landlord asking him to send me my clothes and things, to sell my car if it wasn't too much trouble, and not to hold the house for me. Then I scoured the newspaper for other job listings, in case my application for the guide job was turned down.

On Friday, Thomas Snow called me at Thistle Down House to let me know that the job was mine. "No problems, then?" I said happily.

He hesitated a second or two before he answered.

"One of our members felt the position should go to a girl who had grown up here, rather than to a newcomer. She was very strong on the point you might not be here very long and the job would just have to be given to someone else anyway."

A suspicion had already planted itself in my mind, but I asked, "Who was the member who voted against me?"

"Maybe I shouldn't say, but it was Mrs. Van Orden. And I must say her opinion carries clout with our members. She's the past president of our organization, and her husband's family has been here for generations—well-thought-of people. Colette is a kind, generous person, too," he said, "giving both time and money to better our endeavors. But my opinion also carried weight," he added.

"Thank you, Mr. Snow! I do plan to be here for at least the rest of the summer. This fall I may go to college."

"We've thought of that, but keeping the craft center open when the weather turns colder isn't a likely possibility, so we wouldn't need you then, anyway. We look upon the opening this summer as an experiment. Next summer, we hope you'll return. I felt your experience as a sales clerk in Oregon at J.C. Penney's was in your favor, and we called your employer. He gave you an excellent recommendation. That, and the fact that your family once owned Halic House, swayed the majority of our voting members."

It was odd, but I felt like an impostor and yet entitled to the job, both at the same time. On my off hours, I decided, I would just have to work harder to find the actual proof I was after.

"I'm really happy to have this chance, Mr. Snow," I told him. "And I'd like to thank you for your part in getting me the job. When can I begin? Is the craft center ready for me?"

"It opens next Wednesday. But tomorrow, we'd like you to meet here with Mrs. Van Orden. She will take you through the craft center and explain everything, a kind of training session. You'll also be given a booklet to study. And Colette will take your measurements to have a long dress made for you to wear. Mostly, your job will be to smile and be friendly. I know you can do that! Be sure to be here tomorrow at two o'clock to meet with Mrs. Van Orden. I'll be here to introduce you."

"We've already met," I told him, feeling hollow, "but thank you. Thank you for everything." Why did it have to be Mrs. Van Orden who would show me through Halic House, the craft center, tomorrow? I wondered as I replaced the phone on the hook. *Anyone else* would have been better. With no actual proof yet, I was sure Colette hated me and would do anything to get rid of me. Maybe it was time for a showdown, to find out exactly what Mrs. Van Orden's problem was. If the slightest opportunity came up tomorrow, I decided, I'd grab it.

The next day, I arrived at Halic House twenty minutes early for my appointment with Colette. I'd been too nervous to stay in my room.

For our first hour together, poking into the various sheds and the crafts on exhibition about the grounds, Colette showed me courtesy; she was very civil. But, after a while, I began to sense a growing resentment or some other nameless bad feeling toward me, beneath Colette's good manners and flashing smile. She seemed to *fear* me.

Finally, when I was looking at something else and missed her description of how a windlass works (to lift water up from a well by means of a rope on a spool that was turned by a crank), Mrs. Van Orden was quick to say,

"You still have time to back out of this job, Miss Kinney. There are others who would like to have it, girls well qualified."

I looked at her, moistened my lips, and sucked in a long deep breath. It was time then, I thought. "Mrs. Van Orden, I want this job. I'm not going anywhere. I don't intend to 'back out' of anything. Can you please tell me why my being here in Greendale bothers you so much?"

"I don't know what you mean!" Colette protested with a deep frown.

"Yes, you do. Didn't you write me a note, telling me I should leave town right away? Didn't you make a fuss about where I was parking my car because my *presence* in town, and not my car, was what was really bothering you?"

Mrs. Van Orden paled, and her eyes wouldn't meet mine. "I have no idea what you're getting at. I simply thought you weren't going to be here in town very long. I recommended that another girl be given the job. If you're going to be high and mighty about that, then perhaps the job should be given to someone else."

"You are missing the point," I said, trying to keep my temper. "I'm here to stay. This job is mine. If something about my being in Greendale upsets you, now is the time to tell me about it." I waited, feeling hot and frustrated here in the yard as Mrs. Van Orden stared back, her lips clamped tight.

"All right," I gave in, sighing, after the silence grew unbearably long. "If you're not going to say what the problem is, there's nothing I can do about it. But I do have something to say to you: I'm not here to hurt anyone; that's not what my coming to Greendale is about. I'm sorry if my being here may create some kind of trouble for you. But I definitely don't think it's fair that I remain in the dark—that I go on knowing nothing about myself, just to keep covered some deep, dark secret. I won't run. That's final. I hope you understand.

I had no idea where my courage came from for the outburst. I stood, feeling ill and quivery inside, but glad I'd spoken my piece.

Mrs. Van Orden put her hand to her throat. She whispered hoarsely, "If you'd only go, just *go*—"

"Tell me why?" I pleaded, but Colette shook her head adamantly. "All right"—I shrugged—"I'll be here on the job, Wednesday. Is there anything else you need to show me about the craft center, Mrs. Van Orden?"

"S-such—s-such an upstart!" she sputtered. "Someone else will have to measure you for your dress. Please tell Mr. Snow that I had to return to the gallery." Propelled by her anger, Colette Van Orden whirled stiffly and marched off.

I watched her go, sighing, wishing I could understand.

Too many unfilled blanks made understanding impossible though. I only knew that I could not leave. I had friends here in Kansas: my Fontaine cousins, Mr. Snow, Birdella, and Rom. I was staying. But I couldn't help but wonder, and worry a bit, about what might happen now.

MY FIRST DAY AS GUIDE AND HOSTESS AT THE HALIC House Pioneer Craft Center was not without problems, beginning with my petticoat, which turned out to be too large around the waist. It kept slipping down, threatening to trip me, until, embarrassed, I was able to remedy the situation with a safety pin begged off a visitor to the center.

The first day the children were like gabbling turkeys;

they gave me a headache. I decided I would get used to it in time. Or perhaps I'd learn to keep them more interested and quiet. Luckily, the craftspeople knew their work and could take over explaining their skills and individual crafts. The youngsters seemed to particularly like stringing apple slices for drying (nibbling bites as they worked) and churning butter and candle and soap making.

I felt like a Pied Piper with the children trouping after me, through the Halic House Museum, on to the Pioneer Craft Center, and finally through the orchard and garden to my favorite part: the mill and waterwheel down by the stream, which angled along the property line.

More than once I wished that I might have lived here at Halic House myself, long ago, as Gram had, and Selena and Rosemary. Although there must have been a lot to do, it must have been a simpler, more tranquil time.

TWO DAYS BEFORE THE FONTAINE REUNION, GRACE called to tell me when they would pick me up. Luckily, it was a Saturday, not one of my days at the museum.

On the appointed morning, I was surprised when I answered my door at Thistle Down House to find that Ted Fontaine, rather than Grace, had come for me. I had made up my mind that he would probably find something else to do today. Go out with one of the many girls who were attracted to him, rather than attend a family reunion that could only be dull by comparison. My surprise showed as I floundered. "Ah—hi. It's—you. I thought...oh, bananas!" I wailed, laughing. "It's nice to see you, Ted."

"You had me wondering." A wide grin cracked his tan

face. "Let's go if you're ready. Mom and Dad are waiting for us down in the car."

As we walked side by side down the quiet, carpeted hall to the stairs, I could feel his appraising glance on me, and I was glad I had worn my new white sun dress, which showed off my own tan. In a moment, he reached out a hand to flick the side of my hair back with his fingers. "Pretty," he commented. I felt myself blush, appreciating the compliment. But I would rather have had Rom by my side today than cousin Ted. Grace had said just about everyone from the surrounding communities came to the reunion. Rom might be there, I thought. Shoving down a small ache of unhappiness, I decided it would be smart not to get my hopes up.

Chapter Eleven

Grace embraced me at the curb in front of the Thistle Down as warmly as if I were her daughter. She introduced me to her husband, Jim Fontaine, an older version of Ted in looks, who seemed shyer than either his wife or son.

Mr. Fontaine held my hand and told me, "We hope you find out something about your folks today, but even if you don't, have a good time with us, okay?"

"Thanks." I felt like hugging him, but I was afraid to get my hopes up. Whatever, the Fontaines had predicted a large turnout of people from the area, and I supposed anything could happen.

Grace was trying to usher us a bit farther down the street, to where her bronze Buick waited. "Jim," she called, "we'll take the backseat. The kids can ride in front. Ted, do you still have the keys?"

He jangled them at his mother as he walked me to the passenger side. I slid in, and he went back to climb in behind the wheel. When we were on our way, Grace said, "I want to hear all about this new job of yours, Bryn. It sounds like such a nice thing for you, and for the community, too, this craft center. I can hardly wait to take the tour. I don't want an exclusive tour, either, I want to romp right along with all the little kids." She laughed.

Of course, I laughed, too. I saw that not only Grace, but Mr. Fontaine and Ted looked interested, so, turned in the seat, I went into full detail of my duties as hostess and guide.

"The antics of some of the kids are the neatest part," I told them, finishing up. "One day, there was this little girl who stared at me constantly, as if something was wrong. If I made the least move toward her, she would jump away and stay out of reach. Finally, I realized that because I had been introduced as a descendant of the family, the little girl had taken that to mean I was a Halic reincarnated, *a ghost!* After we cleared it up for her, you never saw a kid so relieved. Even so, I never was able to get her to take my hand that afternoon."

Ted interrupted the laughter, saying, "I like kids. Even thought about being a teacher for a time. But I'll never get farming out of my bones."

"You'll marry a nice girl and then have a raft of kids of your own," Grace soothed from the backseat, reaching up to pat his shoulder.

"Ma"—Ted groaned—"don't get any ideas, because you'll only be in for disappointment. I'm not getting married until I'm thirty-five."

"Or older," his father commented drily.

"Or older! You've got it, Dad." Ted grinned at him in the rearview mirror. "It'll take that long to pick out a girl from the horde that's after my body."

"Stuff it, you conceited young rascal," Grace ordered. "We're flying by all this Kansas scenery," she commented, "when we should be showing it to Bryn. Hon—"

"Ma, Bryn is from Oregon where they have real scenery!" Ted interrupted.

"Horse stuff, we have nice things to see, too. Bryn, honey, have you noticed the stone fenceposts? They're different, aren't they? There's an interesting story that goes with them, too. From the early days, the settlers dug slabs of limestone from the ground to use for fence posts. There were few trees. Spikes were driven into the stone to split it. The limestone is soft when it first comes out of the ground, and it can be sawed. It hardens with exposure. And set in the ground, the posts stand against rust, wind, weather, and time. You'll see posts, and limestone buildings, too, that have been here for more than a hundred years."

"Now wasn't that fascinating?" Ted teased his mother.

"It was," I said. After a while, I told them, "I've never been to a family reunion. I'm wondering what goes on at one. Is it just a picnic?"

"Oh, goodness, no. It's more fun than that," Grace explained. "We have games, like sack races, egg toss, and onion-eating contests." She giggled. "The men play horseshoes, sooner or later. Someone will get a Softball game started. And we talk and talk—make up for the time we haven't seen each other. The picnic tables will nearly fold under all the food. Everybody brings the dishes they make best, their specialties. Until you've been to a Kansas family reunion, you've truly missed out, I mean to tell you!"

Ted looked at me and silently mouthed, as he made a thumbs down sign out of his parents' sight, *"Boring, boring, boring."*

If he really had meant it, then he wouldn't have looked so cheerfully expectant when we approached the picnic grove, later. It was a cool, inviting, tree-filled draw settled among the rolling hills. Ted drove into the grove and let us out near a large gathering of people of all ages who were busily talking, hugging, and kissing in greeting. Then he drove away to find a parking spot out at the roadside.

I watched a spindly girl of thirteen or so and an older graying woman in a hand-waving, excited discussion of horse shows and competitions. Then I realized that I was lagging behind with my carton of 7-Up and the banana crumble dessert I'd made. Grace and Jim were ahead carrying their coolers of food to the tables. I started to run, when a familiar male voice stopped me, "Bryn!" I whirled to face him, and he came running, a wide grin on his face.

As always, seeing him, I was reminded how awfully good-looking Rom was. Today, dressed in white trousers and a melon shirt, dark tan, he knocked me out. And I was instantly aware of how much I cared for him.

Frowning, he shoved his hands in his pockets when he reached me. "If it turns out we're related, I swear I'll kill myself," he joked. "You haven't uncovered evidence that you're a Fontaine, have you?"

"I'm still a Halic-Burgess-Jones descendant as far as I know. I was invited here by my cousin, Grace, a Fontaine by marriage. I don't think we are."

"God, I hope not. See, my grandma was a Fontaine, before she married Grandpa Elliot, so that's way off another bunch, nothing to worry about. But for a second there I was scared you might turn out to be a mysteriously missing twin I'd never heard about, or something equally close. That's not how I'd like to be related to you."

His meaning both pleased and embarrassed me; I was glad when he caught my elbow, his hand curving around it. "I wasn't fair to you that night when I gave you a bad time about tracing your family," he said seriously. "Again, I'm really sorry. I haven't felt right, since. And I've wanted to see you so bad."

"It's okay," I told him. "I was wrong, too." I was trying to think how I might explain myself better, when I was distracted by a teenage couple younger than us, struggling to replace a tablecloth that kept blowing off the table a few yards away. Behind the billowing cloth they sneaked a kiss, then a second one, longer.

Rom saw them too. "Now they've got the right idea." He laughed.

Suddenly, I felt a firm grasp on my waist from behind, pulling me away from Rom. Startled, I saw that it was Ted, the devil dancing in his eyes. He nuzzled me. "I've been looking everywhere for you, honey."

"Ted, don't." I laughed, trying to pull away, but he only held me tighter. I couldn't bear the hurt look on Rom's face as he stared. "Rom, this is Ted Fontaine," I said, twisting in Ted's hold. "He—"

"Hey, it's okay," Rom said with a faked grin. "No explanation needed. I know when the competition has me beat." He started to back off, then he came back to shake Ted's hand, "Hi, Ted." The expression in his eyes was awful as he looked at me. "I didn't know you were here with someone else, or I wouldn't have poured my guts out. The apology stands, forget the rest." His voice sounded hollow.

I had no intention of forgetting one thing he said, and no way would I let him keep the wrong idea about Ted and me. I tried again to explain, "I did come with Ted, but he's—"

"No, no, it's okay," he insisted, his mouth tight.

I figured he had a low opinion of girls who came with

one guy and ditched him for another, and he thought that's what I was doing. Which made me all the madder. Why wouldn't he give me a chance to explain? And Ted only made matters worse, cuddling me close. They were both insane!

Rom cracked his knuckles as he backed off. "You two have fun—"

I watched him hurry away, so choked with anger I wanted to kill him *and* Ted. I turned on Ted as he released me, so angry I could hardly speak, "You! Why did you do that? I could pulverize you! Hit you with this soda. Oh—!" I fumed, stamping my feet. "Do you know what he thinks? Rom is my—friend, and now you've let him think we're here together."

"We are together."

"Ted! Not like that." I looked over my shoulder and saw Rom's wide shoulders disappearing into a crowd out in the field near some horseshoe pits. I could run after him, beg him to listen, but my pride said to forget it for the moment. We both needed some time to think before we tried to get together. I'd catch up with him later, and he'd listen, or else.

"I'm sorry," Ted said, surprisingly sincere. "I thought he was just some guy trying to make a move on you. And honestly, I did want to be with you, today. I didn't know he was somebody special. Forgive the clowning, Bryn."

I didn't look at him. I hadn't really let myself realize how special Rom was to me. Even though the separation since our argument had gone on unbearably long. Today could have been a reunion for us, too, if Ted hadn't pulled his stunt. Hearing the far-off clang of a horseshoe against iron, I half-wished for one to wrap around Ted's head.

Only it wasn't totally Ted's fault. Rom shouldn't have been so quick to jump to the wrong conclusion. But maybe he was super-sensitive since losing his last girl to the Frenchman. I wasn't Pam, though, and if he really cared for me—

As though reading my mind, Ted said, "He ought to put up more of a fight for you. I would have. Then again, maybe he's over there right now thinking of some maneuvers so he can reenter the battle and claim you. I wouldn't worry. Nothing whets a man's appetite for romance like having another guy after the woman he wants. And—"

"Ted, shut up." Too late, I saw that Grace was back and she had overheard me. My face got warm.

"My goodness." Grace looked shocked. "What's going on? What's this scamp been telling you?"

"Nothing." I laughed. "I just—" I shrugged, not knowing what to say.

"We were giving one another a bad time, Mother, fooling around like cousins will," Ted said offhandedly. I was grateful, and when you looked at it that way, Ted was telling the truth. We were spatting like a couple of cousins.

I felt Grace's examining glance on me still. "Just so you two stay friends," she said cautiously. "Now, come with me, Bryn. I want you to meet my older sons and their wives and kiddies. There are other people to introduce you to, too. Ted, you come along and help Bryn have a good time."

He threw me an innocent look that said, Don't blame me, blame her, as he danced into step with us, taking my elbow. I narrowed my eyes at him in fun, feeling a giggle bubbling up inside. The fact that he'd played a mean trick on me didn't make him one iota less appealing.

. . .

THE PARK WAS FILLED WITH PEOPLE. SOME STROLLED about, stopping now and then to shake a hand here, another there, occasionally stopping to talk before moving on. A leaflet, a brief history of the Fontaine family, had been passed around, and it was a white flag fluttering in hands everywhere.

Grace introduced me to so many people that after a while I stopped trying to remember names. And she always asked if people had known Gram and Teal, but no one knew more than I already knew.

At the noon feast, I sat with Ted on one side of me and Grace and Mr. Fontaine on the other. Across the plank table sat the older Fontaine sons, Matt and Gregory, who turned out to be easy-going, friendly young farmers, who kept up an affectionate banter with their wives, Jan and Loretta, and with each other. Matt's towheaded one-year-old son, and Gregory's dark, shy little girl perhaps a year-and-a-half old, rounded out the family. And me. I did feel a part of them, although I hadn't known any of them long.

The brothers and their wives would forget and treat me as Ted's date, though, at times, and he did nothing to discourage it. I let it go, although a part of my mind wandered, wondering where Rom was and how I could approach him and make him listen to me. As time passed, I grew more restless, worried that Rom might leave the reunion and return to the dig, for perhaps more interminable weeks.

After the meal, I refused Ted's invitation to join him in a three-legged race. For some time, I wandered alone among the groups of people, trying to locate Rom, if he was still here. I'd about given up when Grace came rushing up to me, her face flushed and perspiring. "I've had the hardest time finding you!" She grabbed my hand.

"I've found someone, an old neighbor of your grand-mother's, of Ivana's. Her name is Bertha Warren; she's a gossipy old thing, but isn't that what we want?" She pulled me toward a group of picnic tables where several women sat sipping iced drinks after clean-up.

In spite of my preoccupation and worry over Rom, my heart pounded at the idea of meeting someone who had once lived next door to Gram. "Grace, do you think—?"

Suddenly, she yanked me in a different direction. "There's Bertha!" We headed toward a row of portable toilets that had been set up on the edge of the grove. A woman coming from that direction waved.

Grace brought us together. "Bertha, this is Bryn Kinney. We're sure she is Ivana's grandchild, as I was telling you. But we need to know more. Bryn, this is Bertha Warren. She was Ivana's neighbor in Greendale."

Bertha Warren's gray hair was see-through thin, her wrinkled, oatmeal-colored skin hung loose at her throat like turkey wattles. The liveliest part of her was her eyes; they made me think of quick, darting minnows. Blood-thirsty piranhas, actually, from her total expression. But the woman's personality, pleasant or unpleasant, was of no care to me. If she could help me, I'd be eternally grateful. "Hello. You knew my grandmother well?"

"Yes, I surely did," she rasped smugly at me. "That was before I moved to Lawrence to be near my daughter. Yes"—she squinted at me—"you look somethin' like Ivana used to, but more like him, Gamble, her husband. She showed me his picture many times. Good fellow, I guess. Nobody could forget a face like his."

"Anything you can tell me would be welcomed," I told her, although my throat had grown tight and it wasn't easy to get words out.

Grace intervened, kindly. "I'll get us all some iced tea. Sit down, Bryn, Bertha, over here." She led us to some empty lawn chairs in the shade. "We'll just chew the fat the rest of the day. 'Be right back."

As I sat down, I wondered if Bertha Warren really knew as much as she was making out. She was like a toad, swollen with self-importance, and the few people I had ever met like that often turned out to be little more than bags of air. Still, I hoped for some information. Where to begin? I wondered. "You lived next door to Ivana Kinney; could you tell me where the house is so I can go see it?"

"Dearest friends, we were." Bertha was emphatic. "I lived next door to her for over twenty years. That counts for something, don't it?" She laughed harshly. "But our houses aren't there anymore. They were torn down so a restaurant could be built. One they call the Garden Party. That's when I moved to Lawrence, Ivana'd already gone by then."

I gave up on the house and asked her then, "You must have known Ivana's daughter, Teal, too?"

"Oh, sure. I remember Teal clear back to when she was a high school girl. Snippety kind, she was, never mixed well with others, like my girls' crowd. But you know how that kind is. Teal was said to be very smart, but I don't know how true that was. I do believe she considered herself better than everybody else. Couldn't wait to leave town right after graduation."

What she was saying wasn't too different from what I'd already heard from Grace. "Do you know where Teal went?" I held my breath.

"To some secretarial school, I heard. I don't know where."

My spirits drooped, thinking about trying to trace someone who had gone away to secretarial school "somewhere." "Somewhere" could be any one of a million different places. Grace returned with our drinks; she sat back, getting her breath, smiling encouragingly at me. I returned the smile as best I could. "Did Teal come back to Gram's—Ivana's—to visit?" I asked Bertha.

Bertha was thoughtful, looking a shade disappointed that she didn't have a ready answer. "I don't think she came around much," she said slowly, then. "That was a long time ago, but it seems to me that Ivana was alone most of the time."

"What about Teal's friends?" Grace tried to help. "How about boyfriends? Teal was awfully pretty, as I remember. She must have had a boyfriend while she lived here."

"Well, sure, in high school she was infatuated with that Van Orden boy."

"Who?" I tried to ask, but my tongue wouldn't work. I couldn't move, my mind spun dizzily, as I heard Bertha gabbling on.

"...you remember that, don't you, Grace? Everybody thought she'd hooked him. The way they was never apart, people just naturally assumed Teal Jones and Travis Van Orden would marry."

Colette Van Orden's husband! The man in the wheelchair was Teal Jones's high school sweetheart. Now a few things were a lot clearer. But could jealousy alone, from something that had happened so many years ago, make Mrs. Van Orden behave as she did toward me? And exactly where did I fit in? There were so many pieces of the puzzle still lost. Better listen, I reminded myself. "Do you know what happened?" I asked in a near whisper. "Do you know why they didn't marry?" I thought perhaps that Colette had taken Travis away from Teal.

Bertha's forehead puckered. "That was forty years

ago, you know. But, yes, now that I think on it, that gives me the answer. Forty years ago would have been the Second World War. Travis was called to war before they could marry. Just a youngster he was. Sure! And he was reported missing in action—now I remember. You wouldn't have believed the fretting that went on in that house in them days. Teal thought Travis was dead. She got more self-centered than ever, it seemed to me. I guess it was then, and not at graduation, that she went away to secretarial school."

Grace asked Bertha, "Do you know if Ivana and Teal got along? For some reason, Ivana never told Bryn a thing about having a daughter, or any family." I was having difficulty sorting the myriad questions rumbling in my mind, and I was glad Grace was there to speak for me.

Bertha took a long drink of tea, her expression a frantic mind-scurrying. The silence was awful as it went on and on. Then Bertha nodded, eyes gleaming, the wattles at her neck quivering. "There was some trouble, I remember it now!"

In spite of the afternoon's heat, I suddenly shivered. Grace reached over and covered my hand with her own, holding it tight. "So what was it?" she asked impatiently.

"It was when Teal Jones did come home one time. It must have been, oh, in the sixties, I guess. Teal was pregnant, and sick besides that. She came alone, so I doubt if she was married. You know how *that* is." Bertha rolled her piranha eyes. "Teal wasn't a young woman anymore, either. She must have been forty if she was a day. She had the baby, there while she was staying with Ivana. I think they didn't want it known about the baby, but you don't hide a thing like that. Several of us got wind of it—"

"Was the baby a girl?" Grace practically snarled. "Was it a boy or girl?"

"Why a—a girl, I think."

"Can't you be sure?" Grace asked, more in control.

Bertha went blithely on, " 'Twas a girl, I think. Gave that infant such an odd name, as I remember. Sort of Scottish, like Burns, or Burn, or—" Her eye flew open wide, fleshy lids disappearing. "It was *Bryn.* You!"

Tears burned in my eyes, and an impossible knot ached in my throat. I knew. Finally, I'd heard from someone that Teal Jones had had a child, a little girl, and the child was named Bryn. I wasn't sure I wanted to hear anymore, but Bertha seemed to be digging in the recesses of her mind, still, for any further kernel of gossip she could bring forth. Not to lose her importance, too soon.

Into the silence, because Grace now too was wiping her eyes, Bertha said, "There was a blow-up of some kind over the baby, right after it come. Don't know for sure what it was all about, but they all disappeared. If I remember, Ivana went first, with the baby. Just up and took off. When she was on her feet again, Teal left, too. Don't know where any of them went, though."

~

WHEN I COULD GET MY VOICE, I TOLD GRACE, "I'd like to walk around for a while alone. And thank you for t-today." She gave me a fond, worried look before she touched my hand to her lips. I clasped her hand tight before I let it go.

For a long while after, I moved among the people in the grove feeling as if I was in a dream apart. I was numb. *Teal Jones,* then. Teal Jones was my mother. I had my mother's name, but I still didn't know her whereabouts. And I needed proof she was my mother. And yet, hearing, even from a woman like Bertha Warren, who my mother was, gave me a feeling of peacefulness. A grasp on something real and true about myself, that I'd never known before, to hang onto forever. I *was born in Greendale, Kansas. My mother was Teal Jones.*

The rest of it, who my father was, where the Van Ordens fit in, remained to be solved. Where to begin with that, I had no idea. But I would find out. Bit by bit I would know it all.

Chapter Twelve

The reunion became muted echoes as I wandered deeper into the grove, barely aware of what I was doing. What was Teal Jones really like? I wondered. Where was she? Had she changed as much as Gram had, from whatever life had dealt her? Maybe Teal wasn't the single-minded, ambitious person people told me about. By now, for all anyone knew, Teal could be a—a bag lady, wandering the streets of some far-off city. And if I did manage to find her, what would Teal think of *me!* How would she react to the grownup Bryn, not the baby she evidently hadn't welcomed? I doubted she would want to see me.

Enveloped in thought and mixed feelings, I was only partially aware of a sound in back of me. Then my name was spoken, softly, and I turned, my heart tumbling. Rom stood tall and relaxed in the path behind me, yet there was concern in his look. "I'll go away if you want?"

"Don't you dare!" I whispered, then I was running into his arms. "I can explain about Ted," I said, my voice muffled against his shoulder. "And Rom, I've found out who my mother is!"

"I know, I know." He tilted my face to look at me, stroking my chin. "Ted found me; *your cousin* explained his little stunt. And he and his mom told me that you've heard Teal is your mother. I'm so glad for you, Bryn. I wasn't sure if you wanted to be alone, but I came in case you needed me."

"Need you? Oh, Rom—" I lifted my lips to his, drowning in joy as his lips met mine in a long, firm kiss.

"Beautiful Bryn," he said huskily, placing his cheek on mine. "Special, special Bryn." He caressed my hair. "If I could hold you this way forever, I'd be the world's happiest guy."

I tried to answer, but all I could manage was a little hum of contentment. For the longest while, we remained in one another's arms, kissing, until I felt that my watery knees wouldn't hold me any longer. I led him to a log stump where we sat down. I looked into his eyes, *both* of them, beautifully blue and filled with his feeling for me. I whispered truthfully, "Rom, the worst mistake I've made this summer was putting you off to use all my time to hunt down my family."

"The worst," he agreed, his fingertips touching my lips. "Only kidding," he added softly. "You did what you had to. But I admit that my heart's been down at the bottom of the diggings ever since I left Greendale after our fuss. I've suffered horribly; you can't know how miserable I've been."

"I'll make up for the trouble I caused you." I laced my fingers at the back of his head and pulled him down to kiss his brows. Then, the sweet pressure of his lips met mine and could have remained into infinity, but I finally

drew away. "Can we come up for air?" I giggled breath-
lessly. "I think we'd better."

His grin was regretful, but he nodded and murmured,
"Sure." He leaned away and rubbed his hands down over
his face as if to wake himself from a dream. "We should
head back," I told him, getting to my feet. "Grace won't
know where I am, and I don't want her to worry. I've
been gone quite a while. C'mon, Mr. Elliot, walk with
me." I caught his big hands and pulled him to his feet.

Rom slipped his arm about me, and we walked back,
little puffs of dust rising in the path. The warm scent of
nearby ripening grain and wildflowers filled the air. It was
a moment I'd always treasure. I sighed, a little fearful at
the wonder of it.

"I've got the greatest idea," Rom said after a while.

"What?" I smiled up at him.

He kissed my nose, his finger traced my chin, stopping to caress the dimple. "I have to go back to the dig; I
need the college credit. But I can't give you up right away
again, either. Some weekends I can come home and see
you, but this time, how about coming back to the dig
with me? Just for a few days vacation, to get away? How
about it?"

We had stopped in the path facing each other, arms
about one another's waist. From not far away now came
the sounds of the reunion breaking up, people calling
goodbyes, car doors slamming. I looked at Rom, at the
eager wistfulness in his expression. I didn't like the
prospect of being separated from him, either, but there
were problems. "I have a job now," I told him, "I'm a
guide at the new Halic House Pioneer Craft Center."

"So find someone to take your place, please?"

"Actually, I might not have to. We're only open three
days a week. I don't have to be back until Tuesday, but I

should be there then. Getting the job wasn't easy, and I don't want to create any problems for them just now."

"Then there is no problem. You have the next two days off."

"Rom, I want to find Teal. I want to find my mother."

"Sure, I realize that. But do you know how you're going to go about it? Any solid leads?"

I shook my head.

"That's what I thought. Come with me for a few days, relax, enjoy yourself. You'll be out in the wide-open spaces with plenty of time to think. I'll bet you'll come up with something, that way. Okay?"

"You make sense." I laughed. "But I don't know. What will the people at the dig think? Your instructors, won't they mind? And where will I stay?"

"First question: tourists and sightseers are welcome as long as they don't get in the way, or carry off things. You can take pictures, Bryn, give that camera a work-out. Second question: we can take my folks' motor home for you. Nobody's using it. I'll still bunk with the guys." At my hesitation, he added, "I'm not going to push you into anything you don't want. But I feel we should have a chance to get to know one another better, and that's hard to do with me up at Arlington and you here. Besides, I want the love of my life to see what I do."

The whole thing sounded fun and interesting. A good experience and we could get better acquainted. "Okay." I gave him a pat. "Count me in." We continued on.

I saw the Fontaines at the roadside, waiting by the car. Grace was shading her eyes against the sun, looking our way. I regretted worrying my new-found relatives. "Hurry," I told Rom, breaking into a run, pulling him with me. "Grace!" I called, "I'm coming."

Grace surveyed the two of us, a little smile playing about her mouth. "You two found one another, I see."

When I started to introduce Rom, Grace reminded me, "We've already met Romney, hon. In fact, we had quite a talk. I like your young man. And Ted has been scolded good for his little stunt."

Ted shrugged, grinning widely.

"I'd like to drive Bryn back to her place, myself if you don't mind," Rom told them.

Grace chuckled. "I'd say your asking is just a nice gesture, that it's settled already. But just for the record, go ahead. Darling," she told me, "I'll be calling to find out how you're doing. And if there's anything I can do to help you find your mother, find Teal, let me know. In the meantime, I'll try to think of something. We could hire a detective—"

"No," I said, "it's not like she's a criminal. I wouldn't want to do that if I don't need to."

"Take care, then, love." Grace hugged me, then she clasped Rom's arms and gave him a little shake. "You, too." She got in the car. Her husband, Jim, leaned across her to wave at me.

Ted shook Romney's hand. "Take care of my cuz, old buddy." He winked at me and whispered loud enough that even Rom could hear, "Mega-girls hounding me, but you were the pick of the litter. Still are. If you decide to bump the bozo, here, remember me. Distant cousins can marry."

Laughing, I gave him a fond shove in the direction of the car. "Go away! And Ted, be good. I like you, too, cousin." I moved back in the circle of Rom's arm, watching them drive away.

Rom hugged me. "All right, I'll take you back to your room; you can throw a few things in a suitcase. I'll go for the folks' motor home and come back and pick you up. It's quite a drive to Arrington, but turnpike most of the way. We'll get there before it's real late."

The motor home was a wonderful invention, I decided when we'd been on our way for some time. The seats in front where Rom and I sat were as comfortable as living room chairs. In back of us were further comforts of home: a table, padded seats, stove, refrigerator, cupboards, closet, and even a bathroom! It was stupendous.

After a stop at a small country inn for a late dinner, we drove on and on. Every now and then I reached out to touch Rom, his shoulder, or the hair at his temple, his jaw —or just looked at him. It still seemed a miracle that we were together. Occasionally he would lift my hand to his lips, or he'd turn and kiss my cheek. We didn't talk much, didn't need to. I remembered being afraid of him that night he climbed on the bus in Kansas City, and I couldn't believe it now. What a silly little hick I'd been.

A canopy of stars filled the sky, and the moon was high when we finally arrived at the encampment at Arrington. I could make out little but shadows—of other vehicles and tents, as we parked. When the motor was turned off, we went in back where Rom turned on the lights, helped me make up the bed, and draw the curtains at the windows. He showed me the workings of the shower and how to use the stove if I wanted tea or coffee in the morning. Stowed in the cupboard were utensils, towels, and food items.

"Tired?" he asked me gently.

I nodded. "But I'm glad I came. This is going to be fun. I can hardly wait for tomorrow."

"It'll come. Don't get up until you feel like it. When you're ready, I'll show you the place and introduce you around. We all work even on Sunday here. And, hey, if there's anything you forgot to bring, there are other girls who can help out."

I gave him a light kiss and watched him go, his tall frame stooping as he passed through the motor home doorway. I blew him a last kiss when he turned to look at me, then he was melting into the darkness toward a far, shadowy tent. I felt a shade of regret that he was not staying with me, but at the same time, I wanted to be by myself. There was plenty of future ahead of us if that's how things were meant to be. All in good time.

I SLEPT MORE SOUNDLY THAN I HAD FOR A LONG WHILE, and it was well after eight by my watch when I finally, gradually, came awake. I stretched like a lazy cat, thinking to stay where I was a while longer. Then, thoughts of Rom, wanting to be with him and not waste a moment, sent me flying for the shower.

When I was dressed, my makeup on, and my hair combed, a glass of milk and toast waiting for me on the table, I pulled back the curtains to see where I was. The motor home was one of several vehicles lining the edge of a bumpy dirt road. Some distance away, in the center of a rocky, prairie field that was edged on the other three sides by giant yellow sunflowers and a creek, was the dig site. I sat at the table, eating, and took in the view more slowly, item by item, making mental notes of pictures I might get later.

The ground had been scraped bare in an area the size of a tennis court. This arena was then sectioned off by thin rope into squares. Students, sun-browned and dressed in a colorful assortment of hot weather garb, were patiently digging away, a lot like children might at an Oregon beach. One of the guys stood up and peered in my direction. With a quickening of my pulse, I saw that Rom was coming to the motor home, dressed this morning in faded cutoffs and a yellow polo shirt. I doubted if he could see me sitting in the window; it was as if he'd heard my unspoken wish, as he tossed down the tool in his hand to come to me.

I met him at the door. With a huge grin, he reached to grab my waist and swing me to the ground. " 'Morning," he said, catching me to him for a brief second. "Sleep okay?"

"Like a bug in a rug. I'm embarrassed. Everybody else looks hard at work."

"Never mind. I've already explained that you're here to take it easy. To have a look around, and maybe get some photographs. These prairie dogs are great people; they won't object to your being here. Some are so into what they're doing, they may not even notice. So don't be offended if they pay you no attention."

I shook my head. "I'm just glad I won't be in the way." I took Rom's hand and followed him to the site. "Explain everything you can," I told him. "Then I'll leave you alone to work, and I'll go back and get my camera."

"I guess you know the reasons for all this." Rom waved an arm that included the dig site and the students on their knees, absorbed in their work. "These kids have an interest in pre-Kansas history, and this is a form of research. There aren't many written records. Well, there are explorers' diaries, telling about Indians who inhabited this country four and five hundred years ago. Through 'finds' we can help confirm what they said existed back then, and at the same time we can preserve history."

"What are the little red flags for?" I pointed at tiny flags sprouting at random in the bare earth.

"That means an artifact has been removed from the spot. The red flag is placed to record its original location. The pottery pieces, or whatever was found, are sacked and identified here in our laboratory."

I looked around. "Laboratory?"

He laughed. "That's the fancy name for those tables over there under the awning. The kids at the wash basins are cleaning artifacts and cataloging them. It's interesting," he added, "what all you can learn. Like we've found out that these people were far from isolated; they really got around and did their share of trading. Some of the major finds have been glass beads from Europe, obsidian from Mexico, turquoise from the Southwest, and so on."

"I hope you won't think this is a dumb question." I hesitated. "But I don't understand how you know where to dig if there isn't much written about prehistoric times. Why in this place"—I motioned—"and not somewhere else? Or would you be digging any old place you could get landowners to okay it?"

Rom smiled. "Not a dumb question. A site is chosen through a combination of educated guessing and information from those early diaries. Movement of the people can be traced, or estimated. But to be sure of an area, a test is made to prove it's a desirable location. A team will make a study of a potential site ahead of time. They look for a 'mix'—that is, charcoal, bured earth, bits of clay, pottery nor flint, which indicate signs of civilization. The heavier the concentration of 'mix,' the better the location. And naturally, we like to get there before new housing or highways cover history for good. I'll bet this is boring?"

"Definitely not. It's fascinating. It makes me think I might want to do something like this someday, if and when I get into college. Have you personally made any super neat finds?"

"My best one isn't here. Last summer I found most of the skeleton of a man. C'mon." He led the way in the direction of the makeshift lab. "Let me show you this." There, in the lab, on tabletops next to basins, students had carefully laid out bits of shell, pottery, and stone that they had washed.

"Gang, I want you to meet Bryn," Rom introduced me.

He motioned; "Pat, Joe, Brett, Diana, Jeff." They slowed work to say "hi," nodding and smiling, and a couple of them teased Rom about his good-looking new "find." He looked proud but ignored the teasing. "Diana, there, is putting some of the finds into that white glue solution to help prevent further decay," he told me. "When the glue dries, she'll put identification numbers on the pieces for permanent reference."

Rom let me peek into a small bag at the end of the table. Inside were perhaps a dozen blue glass beads. "My find," he told me. "These are European, we're pretty sure. They were probably used in exchange, but they aren't typical wampum—the beads Indians made from shells to use for money and decorations. Let's go out to my little plot, and we'll see if there's any more of them."

For a long time, I watched Rom dig and scrape at the good-smelling earth. Next, he sifted the soil through a mesh screen to catch small or fragmented artifacts. I begged off when he offered me a trowel. "I'm not trained for this the way you are. I might hit some pottery and break it, or miss something I don't know to look for. I like watching you."

Sitting cross-legged in the grass at the edge of the dig, I knew how right Rom was about it being peaceful here.

The hot sun seeped into my skin, burning away care, turning me into softened, pain-free jelly. Why would anyone need pills, when the sun was such a perfect tranquilizer? I wondered.

The sunflowers nodding in the heat only accentuated my drowsy peacefulness, but after a while, I got up and went for my camera. For the next hour, I took photographs of the various aspects of the dig; the site as a whole, specific individuals as they dug, or sifted, or sorted artifacts. I took several pictures of work in the lab. I thought it reasonable that a large number of my shots were zeroed in on Rom, who looked so earnest in his work. He was so deliciously tan and handsome I longed to pester him, but I didn't.

At noon, we lunched together, taking our sandwiches into the shade of a wild elderberry tree. Rom, tired from our long drive of the night before, took a nap with his head in my lap. When he woke he said, "I think you should stay here at least a week, maybe two. Can you?"

I laughed and scolded him softly, "I told you, two days is all. I owe it to the Halic House administrators to be mere now that they've hired me. And there's so much to do. As soon as I can figure out what move to make, I want to continue my search for my mother. I know I can't track down every secretarial school in the state if she went to school here in Kansas. It may have been in another state. If I found the right school, and if they kept records from that far back, they still probably wouldn't know where she went to, from there." I sighed. "It isn't going to be easy."

"It'll all come together, wait and see. You'll find your mom."

He said it so matter-of-factly, I could almost believe him. I leaned down to give him a long kiss.

. . .

THAT AFTERNOON WHEN THE SUN WAS HOTTEST, I stayed inside the motor home with the fan going and read a novel I found there. Rom came for a few minutes during his afternoon break, bringing us iced tea. "Don't worry about me," I answered when he was concerned that I was bored. "Sure it's quiet around here, but I could be paying plenty at some fancy retreat for the same results. I like it here."

That night after a hearty steak barbecue, several students dressed for a movie in town. When Rom asked if I wanted to go, I told him, "If you don't mind, I'd rather stay here and watch a Kansas sunset with you. Maybe go fishing in that little creek over there, if somebody has some fishline and hooks. And watch the stars come out, and talk."

"Agreed! That's exactly what I'd like to do. We can see a movie any old time, but Bryn, until you've seen stars over the Kansas prairie, you ain't seen stars at all."

And, I thought later, if you haven't been kissed by Romney Elliot under Kansas stars, you haven't been *kissed*. He made the night special and exciting, just by being there with me.

We talked until I wondered why our jaws didn't ache. I found out so much more about him, small, personal, funny things. Like the potholders he once made. Potholders! He'd fallen out of a tree when he was little, breaking his leg. His mother, desperate to keep him occupied while he was laid up, taught him to crochet potholders. "God," he said, "I'd never tell a soul but you, but I got to be one hell of a potholder crocheter. I was good! I turned 'em out like you wouldn't believe, stacks of 'em."

I told him about going barefoot the summer I was five, in Oregon, when a bee in the grass stung my toe. In pain, my tongue got tangled and I raced, sobbing, to tell Gram, "I stung my toe on a bee, I stung my toe on a bee." Thinking back, that was one of the few times I'd seen my grandmother come right out and smile. I liked the memory. Stinging my toe on a bee had been worth it.

We were still talking when Rom's friends returned from town, and we would have stayed up all night, maybe, except that his supervisor/instructor urged everyone to turn in for a good night's sleep. Reluctantly, we said goodnight.

Although I thought I would need to read awhile in the motor home to fall asleep, I was wrong. After the day in fresh air and sunshine, I fell asleep almost immediately.

The next day I got more shots of Rom and the other students at work and several close-ups of the enormous yellow sunflowers in bloom around the site. In the afternoon, I walked for miles along the country road, deep in thought about where I stood in my hunt to find my parents. This vast land and open sky made me think of my future, also wide open. In the end, would I be able to fill it with people? There was Rom and the Fontaines, but would I find my mother? Maybe locate my father, too?

Mulling over what I'd heard at the reunion from the distasteful Bertha Warren, I kept coming back to one name: Travis Van Orden. Colette's husband today, but my mother's—Teal Jones's—high school sweetheart long ago. Maybe I hadn't taken Colette seriously enough. The Van Ordens might have many of the answers I was looking for. I didn't know much about them, as people. I headed back for the site that afternoon, hoping Rom could tell me more.

Rom took a break to talk to me when he saw how anxious I was. "Mr. Van Orden, huh?" He scratched his head, then leaned back on his hands where we sat in the grass. "I'd say he's a neat old gent, although I don't really know him. His wife flutters around him a lot, and takes good care of him whenever you see them anywhere. Don't know why he's an invalid. Whatever the cause, their money wasn't enough to prevent it, or help it, I guess. I think Mrs. V.'s art gallery is a kind of plaything for her. I doubt she needs the money. Her husband's family has owned the Van Orden salt mines for generations back. Maybe she works so hard for the good of the town because she can't do anything to change her husband's illness. Helping the town she can do. Just a guess," he said, falling silent.

I liked Rom for figuring people out this way. But there wasn't one item in what he said that I could latch onto and connect with myself, I realized in disappointment. The only way out of it was to talk to them directly. If I couldn't break through to Mrs. Van Orden, then maybe I could get Mr. Van Orden alone and talk to him. I'd rather not be sneaky about it, though, if I could help it.

"They do live in Greendale, don't they?" I asked Rom when it came to me that I'd only seen Colette in town and at Halic House; I had no idea where she lived. "Oh, boy, do they. Nicest place in town, practically what you'd call a mansion. The northeast section of town, on Elderberry Drive. What do you plan to do? Are you going to talk to them?"

I chewed on a blade of grass. After a minute I told him, "I don't know anything else to do. Travis Van Orden was my mother's high school sweetheart. Maybe his wife feels threatened by that, and that's why she acts funny, although I can't imagine why she'd be jealous after so many years. But maybe Mr. Van Orden *has* kept in touch with Teal, and maybe he can tell me where she is."

"Great, I hope so."

It was time to let him know I had to leave. "Rom, you know I have to go back; I can't stay here any longer. I'd like you to drive me into Arlington this evening when you're finished here. I'll take a bus back to Greendale."

He nodded, sighing deeply. Then he looked at me. "You know I'd rather have us together all the time, but I can see how it is, you have to go. Your job, and then you're so close to finding your mom. But why don't I take you back to Greendale in the motor home?"

"And have you driving all night to get back here by morning? No thanks. The bus will be fine. Remember, we met on a bus, so it'll be romantic nostalgia."

"But I won't be there." His grin, though pained, was cute.

"Technicalities," I said, "For what it's worth, I'll be thinking of you every mile. I don't like being away from you, either," I admitted.

"Someday we're going to have to do something about that." He drew me back against him, cuddling me in the circle of his arm.

"Like what?" I teased, but I knew what he meant.

Chapter Thirteen

The direct approach was the only way, I decided at breakfast the morning after my return from the Arlington dig. I'd slept little the night before, worrying how the Van Ordens might react to a visit from me. I wanted to talk to them both at the same time, which meant that I would have to go to their home before Mrs. Van Orden opened the art gallery at nine-thirty, and before I had to report to my own job at ten.

Nervous as I got ready to go, I decided against telephoning first. Mrs. Van Orden would probably only put me off. She might throw me out anyway, I thought. But somehow, I had to make the Van Ordens talk to me. Straight-forward, honest—that's how I'd be, and if they had real kindness in them they'd give me a break.

I almost lost my nerve when I pulled into the private drive at the Van Orden estate, later. The house was intimidating, a magnificent three-storied structure. Victorian, painted a soft dove gray, it was set back in an immense reach of lawns and flowerbeds.

I set off on rubber legs along the brick walk to the

entrance, hoping Mrs. Van Orden wouldn't turn out to be the dragon lady I'd been building up in my mind since our earlier set-to.

A housekeeper answered my ring. I asked to see Mrs. Van Orden, and then waited in the foyer as the housekeeper directed. I felt sick, wished I hadn't come.

Mrs. V. looked preoccupied as she entered the foyer from another room. Seeing me, she stopped. "It's you!" She came forward slowly with her head erect, her hands clasped in front of her. "Is there a problem at the craft center? Why have you come here?" Her voice was guarded, and she looked scared.

And I realized in a crazy panic that I hadn't prepared any opening lines for this. I stammered, "I—I uh, it isn't the craft center. I—I'd like to talk to you *and* to Mr. Van Orden. About Teal Jones." I slowed down. "I understand your husband knew her in their high school days?"

"Get out!" Colette hissed under her breath, looking over her shoulder. "Get out of here this minute. How dare you? To have such nerve, such gall, to ask *me*—"

We stood staring at each other, but I could see that Colette was trying to get herself in control. In a moment, she said very coolly, "I can't imagine what you're getting at, my dear, but you've made a mistake. And my husband isn't well, so I can't allow you to see him. There's nothing we can tell you about the person you mentioned; we know nothing about her. I don't know why you've come here; someone must have given you the wrong information. I'm sorry. Goodbye now." Before I could think what more to say, she had practically pushed me out of the house and closed the door after me.

So that was that. I felt empty as I turned to go back to my car. I fleetingly considered that Bertha Warren might have been wrong about Teal and Travis being a thing in high school, but I knew better. Colette wouldn't have been half as upset if Teal's name didn't mean something to her. Mean a lot. There was nothing left to do but find Mr. Van Orden alone sometime and hope that he would talk to me.

SHORTLY AFTER DAWN THE FOLLOWING DAY, I WENT again to the Van Orden home, parked my car, and walked, in early morning secrecy, the boundaries of the estate. The property covered several acres. The backside was bounded by tall shade trees. A small canal, a man-made brook, crossed one corner of the estate, then meandered on into a city park and beyond. Quaint stone footbridges crossed the brook at intervals along the way.

I could hardly keep my mind on my guide job the next few days as I tried to think of some way to get into the Van Orden home to talk to Travis Van Orden. I could pretend to be a magazine salesperson. Or I could make believe I was taking a survey of some kind, on a day when Colette was at the gallery, of course. But every idea I came up with seemed foolishly out of Nancy Drew.

I took time out for supper, scrambled eggs and asparagus, with Birdella Lamb at her place one night. Luckily, she didn't seem to notice my preoccupation, but chirruped happily *for* an hour or two, with me nodding or answering when I could think to.

On my next day off, I took my camera and went to the park located by the Van Ordens' home. I intended to keep watch on their mansion and come up with some way to get in.

For a while, in the park, I took pictures of little kids at play on the slides and swings and in the sandboxes. There were lots of birds in the park, but none would sit still long enough for me to get a good picture. For the first hour, there was no movement around the Van Orden house and grounds. Then shortly before the lunch hour, I saw Mr. Van Orden coming out onto the back patio in his automatic chair. The housekeeper followed with a small coffee or teapot, which she placed on a table. My heart almost stopped beating in my excitement. I started to walk through the park, taking my time, getting closer and closer to the Van Orden lawn.

I didn't know what I would do.

At the moment Nancy Drew was failing me.

The Van Ordens could have me arrested for trespassing.

A brilliant cardinal flashed by, momentarily taking me off guard. Then, the bird gave me an idea, not a smashing one, but the best I could come up with. On the pretext of following the bird to get a picture, I would wander onto the Van Orden property. When I got there, I would figure a way to engage Mr. Van Orden in conversation.

He sat in his wheelchair with a newspaper spread on his lap, pages of it fallen about the wheels. As I approached, I reminded myself to act normal, casual. I wished I knew a birdcall that might get his attention. But I didn't. Instead, I cleared my throat, loudly. Nancy Drew might be good at this, but I wasn't.

Fortunately, he heard me. He put down the paper he was reading and glanced over his spectacles toward me. I held my breath. This close, I could see how thin he was. In spite of his gray hair, however, I could see that he really wasn't awfully old. When his face broke into a smile, turning up the ends of his silvery mustache, my relief was immense. "Hi," I said.

He nodded, turning to see me better, his arms resting on the chair. "Did you get lost?" he asked in a voice without strength. But he spoke clearly, and his tone was friendly.

I was encouraged further. "Oh, a—not really. I was taking pictures. But the birds won't sit still for me. I particularly wanted a shot of a cardinal. But...I guess I should have stayed in the park."

"Not on my account." He shook his head. "I appreciate the company. That's why I sit out here." He motioned toward the park, where children shrieked joyfully in play. "I get a kick out of watching the kids. I'd have 'em over here to talk with me all the time, but their moms get a little suspicious—and I don't blame them. So I have to be content just watching them. Doesn't sound too exciting, does it?"

"Sounds all right. The kids are neat. I've been getting pictures of them, too."

He nodded. After a moment, he told me, "If you're going to get pictures of birds, you should have a telephoto lens. Don't you have one?"

I shook my head. "I'm pretty new to photography, just learning. I'll get a telephoto lens."

"Here"—he motioned—"let me have a look at your camera." I handed it to him. "You'll have to get something bigger if you want pictures of birds," he said after examining it. "This won't take attachments, it has a fixed lens of its own."

"You—you're interested in photography, too?"

"Photography was my job, once. That was in the Second World War. I'd always been handy with a camera and good with the written word. They made me a front-line photojournalist, eventually. I was carrying a camera, not a gun, the day I got this." He patted his side. "A German bullet with my name on it, in France. I've been fighting trouble from that wound ever since—sometimes on my feet, sometimes not. I've been confined to this chair for quite a stretch, this time. But do you know..." He stared off into space, his expression getting excited. "Do you know," he repeated, "if I could just get back on my feet, what I'd like to do more than anything else in the world?"

I sat down in the grass at his feet, got comfortable, and shook my head.

"I'd pack up all my old camera gear and take off," he told me with a gleam in his eye. "I'd tramp the wilds of Alaska or Africa. And boy-howdy, I'd get me some pictures!"

For a moment or two, neither of us spoke. "Is there a chance of that?" I got the nerve to ask quietly.

"Not much." He shook his head, but he didn't seem bitter. His thin fingers picked at the pleat in his trouser leg. "I saw the war. That ought to've been adventure enough for any man. Sure messed up the rest of my life. I came home in fair shape, from France, with my French bride, Colette, and for a while, we thought I could take over my father's job running the salt mines. That was in the late Forties. I didn't last, I'm ashamed to say. The old war wound kept kicking up. A nephew runs the business now."

"You married a French girl?" I didn't have to pretend interest, I wanted to know about this. I've met her; doesn't she run the art gallery downtown?"

"Yep, Colette is my better half. You see, I was there when the GIs hit Normandy in 'Forty-four. I caught a shell in my midsection, here." He touched his side. "The Germans would have taken me prisoner even though I was more dead than alive if Colette's pa hadn't pulled my bloody carcass into his bakery and hid me out. It was

Colette, just a girl then, who nursed me back to life. She took care of me men, and she still does."

I was trying to think, but I couldn't see how Colette could have known Teal, except by hearsay, rumor. Teal must have been gone from Greendale before Travis brought his war-bride home. Bertha had said Teal hadn't come back often, just that time to have the baby, and then she'd left and had never come back since. I wondered if Teal had other children, a husband and family, now.

"You're awfully quiet, Miss, did I put you to sleep with my dull old talk?"

I shook my head and smiled at him.

"You were interested in taking pictures. Do you want to talk about that?" he asked.

I didn't care, he could talk about anything, just so we got used to one another. When the time was right, I'd ask about Teal. "Maybe you can give me some tips." I looked up at him, squinting against the sun. "I've found that even with a so-called fool-proof camera, I can still get stinky pictures."

He chuckled good-naturedly, his hands patting restlessly in his lap. Then he shook a hand at me, saying, "The photographer makes the difference. *You* take the picture, not that camera, remember that. You control what the camera catches. The composition, the form of the photo, is up to you. Now, most beginners make the mistake of having their subject right in the center of their picture. Don't do that; it's better to have the bird, boat, or kid—whatever you're taking a picture of—either above or below the center of the picture. And you realize that the best pictures have a single point of interest?"

"I've probably read that," I told him, "but I forget

things. It seems there's a lot to remember. I think I need practice, besides some study."

"You'll catch on, dear," he said kindly. "It takes time. Later you may want to move up to a bigger and better camera, with fancy attachments. But it's best to keep things simple at first. You know"—his thin face became suddenly animated—"I'd like to show you some of my albums of the war if you're interested. Some of my best pictures got into *Life* magazine and *Newsweek*. You could bring your mom and dad with you, some evening when you are all free. I'd like to meet your folks. You are new in town? What's your name?"

Besides my name, which he showed no reaction to, I hardly knew what else to tell him. "I'm here in Kansas by myself," I went on after a hesitation, "on an extended stay from Oregon. I've about decided to make Greendale my home, now. And I would love to see your photographs. Maybe you can give me more good tips at the same time." I got to my feet. I'd gotten the break I wanted, but I wouldn't push my luck too far, I decided. It was lunchtime. It would be my scalp if Colette came home from the gallery for lunch and caught me here.

"You're not leaving?" Mr. Van Orden protested in high-pitched disappointment. I looked at him, not very surprised. My association with Birdella had shown me how lonely some people were, had taught me how much I'd like to change that whenever I could. I hesitated.

"Sorry," he apologized then. "I'm being selfish. Of course, a young thing like you has better things to do than visit with a broken-down old man like me. I just thought maybe you'd talk to me about Oregon. Tell me about yourself. I've been doing most of the yammering. That's a bad habit I've gotten into from not getting out into the swim of things much."

I grinned helplessly and sat back down. "Just a few minutes more. I do like talking to you. You want to know about Oregon?" So I began telling him the things I thought he'd like to know: Oregon's scenic beauty, the waterfalls, mountains, the magnificent Douglas fir trees that timbered the hills. I described Oregonians' favorite recreations: fishing, hunting, skiing, camping. I could tell him from first-hand experience about the lush Willamette Valley where I'd lived, where cherries, strawberries, and many other kinds of fruits and vegetables were so abundant that even the poorest people could have them on their tables.

"After living in a place like that, it seems strange that you'd come to Kansas for a vacation," he broke in, chuckling. "Just come for a change of scene, huh? Well, you got that. Lots of flat, windy, nothingness out here, but I like it, always did. It's home. Then there's Colette, my wife; she gave up her homeland for me. She's kind of a fish out of water here; the gallery helps keep her happy."

Reminded of his wife, I couldn't help getting to my feet again. "I really should go. But I'd like to come back again. Some of my ancestors came from around here, and I'd like to find out if you knew them." There, it was out, for better or worse, to help me or not.

"Tomorrow be too soon?"

I shook my head. "Not too soon. I'm off work tomorrow. I'm the guide at the Halic House Pioneer Craft Center." I was about to tell him that my grandmother lived at Halic House as a child when a cry from the direction of his house made both of us turn to look. Colette Van Orden strode toward us, looking ready to explode.

I shivered in spite of myself. I felt glued to the ground.

"What are you doing here, bothering my husband?"

Colette said in a flat voice. I could see mat she was containing herself for her husband's benefit.

"I'm not bothering ... I'm sorry ..." I stammered. My mind grabbed for words, logic, an excuse. "I was in the park and I came over here to talk to Mr. Van Orden. He's been kind enough to give me some advice about using my camera," I blustered, feeling hot, terrified.

"Travis is ill!" she said. "He has little enough strength, and when someone tires him, it only makes matters worse."

Before I could apologize again, Travis Van Orden said in a weak but angry tone, "Good grief and potholes, Colette! Leave the nice young lady alone. I've felt better this morning chatting with Bryn than I've felt in ages. How many other kids her age would give a cracked-up old veteran like me the time of day, even?"

"You don't realize—" Colette began under her breath, but she didn't finish. It startled me to see her eyes film over with sudden tears, and I didn't know if it was because she thought of me as a danger to him, or because he had yelled at her.

Maybe there was another way to find out about Teal. When I'd told Colette earlier that I hadn't come here to hurt anyone, I meant it. And if my seeing Mr. Van Orden was bad for him, I wouldn't do it. "I'm sorry if my being here is a problem. I guess I'd better not come back, Mr. Van Orden."

Travis was emphatic. "Now this is silly; of course you'll come to see me. Didn't you want to look at my albums?"

"Well, yes, but—"

"No buts, a promise is a promise." He smiled. "Come in the morning. It isn't often I have a captive audience." He looked up at his wife's grim face, winking at her. "It'll be fine, sweetheart. You've got to stop being such a broody hen. Give me a break, some 'space' as the kids put it."

I thought she'd argue, that she might come right out, finally, with her problem over me, but she didn't. "See you tomorrow," Travis called, waving as he set his chair in motion, heading for the house. Colette hurried to keep up with him, looking as if she were biting her tongue. She gave me a last cold glance over her shoulder, but she didn't say that I couldn't come back. Some of my fear eased away.

I knew it was Colette Van Orden the second I heard the knock at my door that evening. "I must talk with you." She was all starch.

"Sure." I gave her the chair by the desk, and I sat cross-legged on the bed, trying to look as though getting bawled out was something I was used to and didn't mind; but inside I felt a chill.

"My husband won't listen to me; he insists on seeing you tomorrow." Her voice made it clear what a disaster that could be. "I don't know what you did to impress him so—I suppose the interest you showed in his photography made him feel useful. He wants to teach you what he knows. And I can't deny him what makes him happy."

"Fine. Then I can see him?" I felt relieved as well as surprised.

"On my conditions only! I won't have him taxed. You mustn't come often, or stay long when you do. You must not tell him any sort of thing that would upset or shock him." She hesitated, giving me a long look as if to make sure I understood. "His struggles to stay alive, the endless operations he's had to endure have left him with a severely weakened heart. A shock might kill him." Her chin lifted and there was fire in her eyes. "I love my husband more than life. He's mine. I brought him from death, once. I will go on keeping him alive, no matter what!"

"Do you realize you're asking me to keep a secret when I don't know what the secret is? That's hard. What is it I might say that would hurt him so much? It has to do with Teal and you and him and me, but *what is it?*

Colette looked at me coldly. "I refuse to put into words what I've tried for years to forget. Eventually, since you persist so stubbornly, you'll know for yourself, but you won't hear it from me. And you must agree never to tell my husband you came to Greendale to find family; if you breathe Teal Jones's name to him, you won't see him at all. You must promise not to do that."

I couldn't say anything for a long time. I picked at the buckle of my sandal. If what Colette said was true, and dredging up the past would cause Travis pain, I couldn't see how I could do it. At the same time, I wanted to hear from him about Teal, my mother, whatever he knew. I wondered if he might sometime tell me things of his own accord that would turn out to be helpful. That surely wouldn't hurt him, and it wouldn't be my fault. I realized Colette had said something I'd missed. I looked up, "I beg your pardon?"

Her eyes flashed. "I said I was willing to pay five thousand dollars for your silence."

"That is disgusting! Forget your money—" I snapped, finding it hard to believe she would go to such limits.

"Then I have your promise without it?"

"Yes, you have my promise," I steamed. "I won't do anything to hurt Travis. Now, I think you'd better leave!"

Chapter Fourteen

laying it safe from all angles, in the following
weeks I only went to the Van Orden home when
Travis invited me. At no time did I bring up
Teal's name, nor did I mention my reason for coming to
Greendale. Together, after his housekeeper let me in, we
pored over his albums: endless scenes of horror and
heartbreak: wounded helping wounded; haggard young
men hardly out of their teens digging trenches in far-off
soil; scenes showing flame and smoke over cities, villages,
and the sea.

My antidote for all that bloody war was to bring him
other books, photojournalists' accounts of explorations
in the wilds of Africa and Alaska, the sort of thing he'd
wanted to do. I couldn't help wondering how Travis had
stood the war, how he could stand reliving it now. Then, I
realized that the only active adult life he'd known was
capsuled in the war years. He had fought for his country
with a camera and with writing; why wouldn't he be
proud and want to remember? He didn't have much else.

With remarkable recall, Travis could often tell me just how and why he got a particular shot. I felt I was learning from him, although, God willing, I would never take such photos.

I showed him some of the pictures I'd taken since meeting and talking with him. He said the pictures were good, that I had an astonishing knack for catching on. We discussed the possibility of my studying photography on a serious basis, possibly making a career of it. I wanted to be really good. I wouldn't hunt with my camera, as he'd wanted to; rather, I would take pictures of people, pictures that would tell stories.

"Did I tell you about the day I joined up?" he asked, near the end of one visit.

I'd gotten to be really fond of Mr. Van Orden, and I knew the feeling was mutual. On more than one occasion, he'd told me how much happiness my visits brought him. "I don't think you've told me." I smiled at him. "But I'll bet you weren't very old when you went in." Seated on a couch across from him in the Van Orden library, I settled back to listen.

"I was eighteen when the Japanese bombed Pearl Harbor, December seventh, nineteen forty-one. I'll never forget that day. Nobody thought the Japanese would bomb *us*. We couldn't believe it. We kept our ears glued to the radio all that Sunday. I'd had other plans, most of us did, but I put 'em behind me and joined up as soon as I could, to help my country end the war, quick." In a while, surprisingly, he closed his eyes and began to hum a slow, lovely, lilting tune.

I waited a moment before I asked him, "What's the song you're humming? It's beautiful."

"The name of it is 'I'll Walk Alone.' It was at the top

of the charts," he said, husky-voiced with nostalgia. "A favorite of the GIs and their sweethearts that they had to leave behind."

"Did you have a girlfriend you had to leave behind?" It seemed a logical question to ask, and although I knew exactly what I was doing, I couldn't see how it could harm.

"Oh, yes," he nodded. "I had a girl all right. We'd been sweethearts all through high school. Boy did we have plans. Both of us were what you'd call high achievers, in school. We intended to go on to college, and eventually I'd take over the family business. We decided to put those plans on hold, though, and I signed up."

I thought, my hopes taking a nosedive, that that was all he was going to say, he was quiet for so long. I ached to ask questions about Teal. I wanted to know how she wore her hair, where they went on dates, her favorite color—anything and everything. But I couldn't see how to ask without getting into trouble. The many personal questions on the tip of my tongue would only serve to make him suspicious.

Suddenly, he said, "I remember the day I left, my girl went with me to the train. God, I didn't want to leave her, then." He looked at me with tears in his eyes. "We were just kids. She was the most beautiful girl in school, although I don't think she knew it. She was a loner, never ran with the pack. She was different, one of a kind. And I loved to show her off, tooling around town in my blue 'thirty-eight Chevy convertible."

"It must have been hard, leaving her," I said, my own eyes getting watery watching his face.

His voice stayed deep. "Teal was my first true love." At the mention of her name, it was all I could do to sit still and say nothing. I bit my lip, waiting for more. "We were going to get married, my Teal and I," he said. "We probably should have. But I was over there in the war—and—she was here. In the meantime, I'd met Colette; her family had taken me in—what they could scrape together of me. I wouldn't have survived without them. I—we—Colette and I got married, and she brought me home to Kansas." He brushed his hands across his eyes, shaking his head.

"Are you all right?" I asked him, afraid.

He smiled at me, "I'm fine. But those memories—with not a few regrets—do hurt."

"We don't have to talk if you don't want to."

"I want to."

"All right." I took a deep breath, trying to keep the emotion I was feeling from my voice. "Did you ever see Teal again? What became of her?"

"She waited for me all that time. She thought I might have been killed, but still she waited. When I finally did come home, I had—Colette, my wife. I hurt Teal, and I didn't intend to. She never married that I know of. At least she hadn't when I ran into her again, years later. Must have been about twenty years ago. I'd flown to Kansas City for a treatment; she was there on business." He shook his head. "We'd changed, we were so much older. She had the career she always wanted, and I was married." He looked at me, his voice almost disappearing. "There was no going back then, even if we'd wanted."

"She was probably happy in her career," I told him. I remembered that Bertha Warren had said Teal had gone to secretarial school. "Was she a secretary?"

Travis's mood lightened and he chuckled. "Not exactly, not at that time. Teal was a go-getter, that girl. She worked her way up to the top. Became an executive for a Wichita aircraft plant, Trans-Wings Aircraft." He laughed again. "She probably owns the company now."

"In other words, you think she's still there?" It was almost impossible to hold my voice steady. My entire body felt like shrieking—with triumph, rage, fear, a horde of feelings I wasn't allowed to let go of.

But fortunately, Mr. Van Orden wasn't aware. "Oh, she's still there, I'm sure. One time when I was feeling down, as if life was hardly worth having, I almost called Teal. She never married I'm sure; she's in the phone book under her maiden name."

My mother had been no further away than Wichita these past weeks, and I hadn't known. *Wichita.* In a state of numbness, I got through the rest of the visit. There were so many things I wanted to say to Mr. Van Orden, a multitude of questions buzzed in my mind, but my tongue was tied. I had promised his wife. Not in so many words, but I had agreed not to let Travis know that Teal Jones was my mother. Nor could I reveal the other ideas that haunted me the rest of the visit.

It was a thought that had skirted the edges of my mind for some time, and now I faced it: Travis Van Orden was likely my father. He had said he and Teal had met again in Kansas City about twenty years ago. I guessed it was more like nineteen years ago, nine months before *my* birth. This was the real reason Colette tried to buy my silence. She knew about me somehow, but Travis didn't. Teal Jones, herself, was the one who'd have to tell me the truth.

THINKING ABOUT ALL OF IT, I TOSSED AND COULDN'T sleep that night. I got up twice to see if the air-conditioning in my room had quit, knowing that wasn't the real reason for my misery. At one a.m. I got up and went over to the kitchenette for a snack, only to find nothing sounded good to eat. I went down to the front porch and sat in the moonlight.

The answers were close, I knew it. I had only to face Teal in Wichita to gain the final pieces to the puzzle. I wondered why I wasn't dying to meet her, now that I knew her whereabouts; then I knew it was because I was scared. Of all the people involved in my *being*, Teal was the most closely connected. She was my mother. She had carried me inside her body, had given me life. But then she'd rejected me long ago, and she might again. I wasn't a fool for punishment.

And besides, I knew the truth about myself now; and I didn't really have to know more. I knew with small doubt that my mother was Teal Jones. I knew where I was born, Greendale, Kansas, on March 6, 1965. More than an inkling told me that Travis Van Orden must be my biological father. I'd found my past; I had a heritage.

So why not let it go? My digging this summer, both inside and outside myself, had made a difference. The insecure little mouse who'd climbed aboard a plane for Kansas in the spring had changed. There was a new assurance in me that I could feel. I was a whole lot less apt to let others push me around. Knowing who I was, what I was, what I wanted to do, knowing I had a background, helped. I had a sense of being real, being whole, complete.

Would talking to Teal matter, would putting myself through such an ordeal change anything? Back in bed, I lay very still and faced the truth, knowing I'd find the courage for what I had to do. Because, deep down, I wanted to see Teal; had to. I was curious, for one thing; I wanted to know what my mother was like as a person.

And I knew I'd never be content until I heard from her why she hadn't kept me, loved me. Why a bitter, silent old woman had been the only family I'd known for all my eighteen years.

I knew chances were good that Teal would refuse to see me. That she wouldn't want me barging into her life after all this time. But I had to *try*. However I looked at it, Teal, at the very least, owed me an explanation.

For a few hours after making up my mind, I slept. Soon after breakfast, I dressed for travel. Smiley grinned at me to "Get on with it" and I told my old childhood friend goodbye. In a short time I was driving southwest, following signs to the turnpike, then toward Wichita. Again I thought how ironic it was that Wichita, where Teal had evidently lived for years, was only forty-odd miles from Greendale, where I was spending the summer.

Before I left, I had found Teal's phone number and address in the Wichita directory. A couple of times I'd tried to dial the telephone number and had chickened out. So I decided to just get into the Celica and drive to Wichita and take it from there. Let happen what would happen after I got there. I was afraid if I didn't go today, I might not have the courage again.

The forty miles to Wichita were quickly covered as traffic pushed me along. I gripped t wheel and sat forward as more and more cars filled the highway approaching Wichita. The city ahead of me was Kansas's largest, more than ten miles across. I probably wouldn't be able to find my way around. I wished I could switch directions, heget off the turnpike. As it was, I nervously turned with a stream of traffic, taking the George Washington Boulevard into the city.

As soon as I was able, I took a side street and then pulled off into a parking lot behind a restaurant and stopped. I sat trembling, staring at the back entrance to Antonio's Italian Restaurant where two cats prowled a row of garbage cans. I closed my eyes, hurting in the morning sunshine, and pushed down in the seat to think. I needn't have come so early, I knew. Teal would be at her office, and I wanted to see her at home. That would be best.

I decided to leave the car for a while, walk around some, get my bearings and plan my meeting with Teal. I'd get a city map from somewhere and possibly ask someone to give me directions. I had all day.

For quite a while, I walked up and down the streets of the city, gazing into shop windows, my mind a blank when I needed most to figure things out. I went to a diner and had a glass of milk and a gigantic chunk of coffee cake, which I almost swallowed whole from nerves. I was given directions to a print shop a couple of blocks away where I could buy a Wichita city map.

The owner of the shop, a short, paunchy man who wore a visored cap above a face so filled with lines it could have been a map, too, offered to help me find the address I was seeking. With ink-stained fingers, he took the slip of paper from me, with Teal's address written on it. He peered at it, and his eyebrows went up. "Ritzy," he said. "Your friend lives in a nice part of town, way over northwest between the Arkansas River and the Little Arkansas. It won't be hard to find. We deliver copy over that way once in a while." He scribbled further directions around the edge of the map. "There you go." He handed it to me. "Welcome to Wichita."

Fortunately, there wasn't a ticket for illegal parking on my car when I got back to it. I climbed in and went over the map and the printer's handwritten instructions twice more, then I turned the key in the ignition, fairly sure I could find Teal's place.

~

HER ADDRESS TURNED OUT TO BE A CONDOMINIUM, part of Elyria Village, one of numerous rose-brick and glass two-story townhouses. Very modem, classy, Townhouse decks overlooked the river. I drove by several times before I finally parked the Celica in a tree-planted park across the street from Elyria Village. Robotlike, I got out of the car. Knowing full well that Teal would probably be at work and not at home, I crossed the street and took the walk to her front door, where I mechanically rang the bell over and over. Now that I was here, I hated the wait ahead of me. I wanted to see Teal, now. But as I'd expected, no one answered my ring.

Teal could be out of town, I realized. She might not come home today, at all. But I would wait until evening to find out, and if I didn't make contact with her tonight, I would come again, and again. The drive from Greendale to Wichita was short enough.

I wandered the afternoon away, seeing as much of the town on foot as I could. Teal's home city was more cosmopolitan than other Kansas towns I'd been to. I ate a salad bar lunch at a small cafeteria in a shopping mall. I bought magazines in a bookstore, and I finally returned to my car to read. Because of my lack of sleep the night before, a couple of times I almost dozed off. Those times I got out of the car and walked again.

At four-thirty by my watch, I left the car and walked to a nearby park restroom, where I reapplied my makeup and fixed my hair. The white face that looked back at me from the mirror, the scared eyes, didn't look like me.

I began to stroll back and forth in front of the entrance to Elyria Village, watching expensive cars pull into and out of the townhouse garages as the dinner hour neared. People came and went, sometimes a gentleman alone, or a well-coiffured older woman with two or three lookalikes in her car, and a few younger couples. None of the women looked the way I thought Teal might, and her garage stayed empty.

There was a lonely ache inside me as the day waned and the sun started to sink west of the city. Tired of walking in front of the Village, I returned to my car. When I looked up, later, I saw a small sports car pulling into the main drive at Elyria Village. I watched, holding my breath. The car disappeared into the garage at Teal's unit. I wondered if I should wait a few minutes. Then, I knew I couldn't.

I felt calm, although I'd developed a ridiculous case of hiccups. I locked my car and crossed the street to Teal's condo. I pushed the doorbell. Anxious, I rang again. Then the door opened, and a woman stood smiling at me. "Hello?" she said again. She was small and exquisite in a pale peach linen dress. My hiccups vanished as I stared into smoky-lashed, deep blue-green eyes that watched me with patent amusement. "May I help you?" she asked when I still hadn't said anything.

"T-Teal?" I swallowed to rid the cottony feel in my throat. "T-Teal Jones?" A small frown wrinkled Teal's brow, and I knew I must have sounded as strange as I felt. Her hand went up to her hair, which was gray at the temples. I wanted to say who I was, but I was afraid of having the door slammed in my face before I could say enough.

"I'm Miss Jones—Teal," she answered slowly. Her voice was low and husky, not crisp and sharp as I would have expected it to be. She waited with one hand on her hip, the other dangling a pair of sunglasses.

"I'm Bryn Kinney," I blurted. "I have to talk to you."

Teal's frown deepened, but she looked puzzled and shocked rather than angry. "You're Bryn?" Her lips parted, and I could see a nervous fluttering of her pulse at her throat. Then she shook her head. "This must be a joke. Someone has put you up to this—?"

"I'm Bryn Kinney. This isn't a joke unless you consider your own daughter a joke." My voice was giving out on me.

Teal stepped outside, holding the door closed behind her. "I don't know who you are, or who put you up to this, but it isn't funny," she said angrily. "I have a dinner engagement, and I haven't time for nonsense. Now, do you want to tell me who you really are and what you want? You have ten seconds!"

"That's hardly enough time!" I retorted hotly, without thinking. "It's taken me my whole life to find you, and it hasn't been easy. I told you, I'm Bryn. And I'd like to talk to you, but if you don't have the time—!" My voice caught on a sob.

Teal Jones leaned back against the door as if unable to hold herself up. She wet her lips. "You're not kidding, are you? You are Bryn. But you'll have to show me proof."

Tears scalded my eyes, and I began to laugh hysterically. "Proof? You're asking *me* for proof? I'm the one who has wondered all my life who I am. You knew. You could have told me at any time. *You* need proof?" I put my hand to my mouth, trying to control the violent sobs that shook me.

"Oh, my God," Teal whispered. "Oh, my God." Tears filled her eyes. She took my hand. "Come inside. We can't go on like this out here." She pushed the door open and led me inside. "I must meet someone in less than an hour," she said, "but we'd better get this straightened out. How did you find me? Is Mother here in Wichita with you? I never dreamed either of you would ever care to find me."

"I found you by myself. Gram is dead," I told her. "I don't have to stay this time if you're rushed. But I do have to talk to you, and it may take more time than you can spare this evening."

Teal stared at me, her features frozen. Then she shook her head as if to clear her mind. "I'm being stupid. Forgive me. I'll cancel my date. After all, it's been eighteen years since I've laid eyes on you, hasn't it? We'll talk."

I sagged in relief and found my way to a huge beige sofa as Teal hurried into her bedroom to make her telephone call. I wasn't sure it had registered with her that Gram was dead. Unable to sit still, I got up and went to a big window. Below me were sculptured gardens, a swimming pool, and far in the distance smoggy miles of airports and terminals. Teal's livelihood. I guessed that it was she who sent the support checks over all those years, the money that Gram wouldn't use.

Teal looked even more shaken when she came back into the living room, and I knew it was because she'd had a few minutes to think. I'd upset her, but I felt the worst was over. She was going to hear me out, and I was thankful for that. Teal sat down rather suddenly in a large curved chair, leaning back as she surveyed me across the room. "You'll have to give me a minute," she said, her fingertips pressed to her temples. "This is a shock. I never dreamed—"

"I would have called, but I was afraid you wouldn't see me if you had advance warning," I told her honestly.

She shrugged, "I don't know what I would have done. but now that you're here...Did you say Mother is—is gone?"

"Gram died this past April," I said through a dry throat. "It was sudden, she didn't suffer, like from cancer or anything."

Teal was close to tears, and she spoke more to herself. "I wonder if she ever forgave me?"

I didn't want to be unkind, but I felt I should be honest. "I don't know what took place between the two of you, why there wasn't any communication. I only know that Gram remained close-mouthed, cold toward people, to the end." If I'd known a kinder way to say it, I would have, because I felt Gram had suffered enough in her lifetime. Now that I knew about her, I didn't want her memory tarnished, too.

As though she was on my wavelength, Teal said softly, "Mother was a strange one. Now—now she's gone. It's so hard to take in, you'll have to excuse me." She wiped her eyes with a tissue she held in her hand. Her face seemed to lose some of its sophistication as her feelings showed. Earlier, in her elegance, she could have been any age; now she looked her fifty-nine years. "I think I'll have a little sherry." She cleared her throat. "May I get you some?"

I shook my head.

"Not that sherry will help much," Teal said as she poured a glass at a portable bar at the far end of the room. "I've never found liquor to be much help for anything." I got the idea that she wanted to talk, but for the moment she wanted to steer clear of our main conversation. "Lately, I've been trying to escape the corporate Ferris wheel. I quit smoking." She looked at me, "How about you, Bryn?"

"So far, I don't drink or smoke. I'm not very worldly.

I've only just recently broken out of my shell and learned to do things on my own."

Teal nodded. "A boyfriend, I suppose?"

I couldn't help smiling, in spite of the tension in the room, just thinking of Rom. "Yes. A very neat guy, Romney Elliot. I met him here in Kansas. He's an archaeology student."

Teal came to sit beside me on the couch. "I don't know what to say to you, Bryn. I'm not sure what you're here for, what you expect of me. Needless to say, I wasn't prepared for this—meeting you."

"Ever?" I asked more sharply than I meant to. "You never expected to talk to me face to face, ever? Didn't you want to? Didn't you care?"

Teal jumped up, her blue-green eyes flashing. "Now, just a minute," she protested. "We're getting on shaky emotional ground. There's a lot you can't possibly know. I do want to talk to you, Bryn. But let's take our time. I'm still trying to decide how I feel about your being here. I think I'd like to get to know you, but please, one step at a time. Now, for the record, I've worked incredibly hard all my life to get where I am today. Being a parent wasn't part of my plans." At my small outcry, she hurried on, "Even so, yes, you were born. And I have thought about you, often. But Mother would never have allowed me within an inch of you."

"OKAY!" I shouted. *"That's* what I want to talk about. Why wouldn't Gram let you see me? I'm your daughter. What was the fight about? Why would she keep me from you? I'm really sick of all this hidden stuff and these secrets."

My outburst could have caused Teal to show me the door, but instead, she smiled sadly. "Slow, Bryn, let's take it slow, remember?" She straightened, looking in control as she said, "I'll finish my sherry, but I'm famished. I doubt that you've had dinner, either. Shall we go out to eat, talk, and get better acquainted?" She cautioned then, "But until we get a little more used to one another, let's go easy on the heavy stuff, okay?"

"All right," I agreed, willing to go along with anything as long as she'd have me.

Chapter Fifteen

The restaurant Teal took me to was small and plain, but had a quiet richness that made the Garden Party seem a greasy spoon by comparison. I tried not to stare now that I was up close to Teal, but it was hard.

I had thought about Teal so much this summer, wondered about her, so it wasn't as if I was sitting with a complete stranger. It was as if I already knew her but needed to know her better.

In spite of myself, I found that I was looking hard at each feature of her face. Her eyes, nose, mouth, ears—looking for resemblance to my own features. Teal's eyes were shaped very much like my own but were not the same color. Our ears, sort of elfin-shaped, were similar. I looked away when Teal caught my wide-open stare. "I—I'm sorry."

But she laughed, admitting, "Don't think I'm not curious about you, too. So it's all right. I suspect we both feel pretty strange right now. For openers why don't you tell me about Oregon, where you went to school, friends, that sort of thing, so I can catch up."

"There isn't much to tell that's interesting. I was a good student, above average, I guess. I plan to go to college. I like history, literature, journalism, art." I heaved a sigh, deciding to tell it the way it was. "I didn't have many close friends. Gram and I were different, kind of— outsiders. She could be pretty rude to people; she made it clear she wanted us left alone. And that's how it was. There weren't many kids who'd bother to sort me out for a friend; I was quiet, plain. And I didn't have all the goodies other kids had—nice clothes, a bicycle. Most of my life we lived in a decrepit old store buil—"

Teal's eyes had gone wide with disbelief. "That can't be!" She sat forward. "You've got to be kidding, because I sent support money. It should have covered *some* things. I sent support from the time I located you in Oregon till this spring..."

"Gram didn't touch it. She put every penny in the bank in trust for me. And I didn't know about it until after she died and the bank let me know."

"No." Teal shook her head. "This can't be. I wanted to help you both. She couldn't have hated me that much." Her hand went up to cover her mouth. Moments later, when the waiter arrived to take our order, she blinked away tears and was quickly herself, smiling. "Th-the veal, please, and a salad. Bryn, the same?" I nodded.

When the waiter had gone, I told Teal, "I'm sorry this is upsetting to you, but if I tell you how things really were, the truth, I can't make it sound happy and pleasant when it wasn't." I didn't mean to hurt, but I added, "If I ever have children, their lives won't be like mine if I can prevent it. The happiest I've ever been has been this

summer, finding out who I am, finding where my ancestors came from and— Rom."

"I'm glad things are better for you now." Teal tried to
smile. "Thank God. I was beginning to feel like an ogre, a
monster, for the way your childhood went. But I certainly
didn't intend—didn't know—" She fell silent, and I could
see she was blaming herself, and possibly trying to think
what to do about it.

"If I haven't given as much thought to you as I should
have, I want to now." She was looking at me as if for the
first time she was seeing *a person,* rather than a vague
minor obligation. "I've been much too much into my
work." She shook her head. "God, I can't believe I hadn't
given any thought to your college education till this
minute. I'm so sorry."

We ate, and from time to time we switched to other
topics, as though by mutual agreement we had to have
intermissions to survive this first evening together. She
told me about her work as vice president of the aircraft
plant— most of it too complicated for me to understand.
I told her that I was working in the Halic House Craft
Center. I talked further of Rom, tending to go on rather
glowingly, but I couldn't help it.

"He sounds darling, a wonderful boy. Is he as perfect
as you make him sound?" Teal teased.

"Perfect for me." I grinned.

Teal studied empty space for a moment, then she
turned back to her meal. "I remember being that crazy
about a boy, myself when I was your age."

I took the plunge, unable to stop myself. "I've met
him, Travis Van Orden."

She stared at me, the blood draining from her face.
"You've met Trav, but he's—" She stopped.

"We're good friends," I told her. "He's taught me

about photography. I take him books, keep him company, try to cheer him up since he isn't able to do the things he'd like, more active things. He's my father, isn't he?" It was out of me before I realized that I was saying it.

Teal seemed to be gathering a forced calm about herself. "We'll finish this conversation back at my apartment," she said matter-of-factly. "You must know this is like a nightmare for me. First, you rum up. I find out that Mother is dead, and now you ask—" She shook her head, reaching for the check. "I'm going to tell you everything you want to know, Bryn. I owe you that and more. Only —not here. This is too much for me all at once, and I don't intend to fall to pieces in public."

I didn't disagree. But I wouldn't have cared if we flooded the whole state of Kansas with our tears, just so we got everything out in the open.

BACK IN HER APARTMENT, TEAL DIDN'T BEAT AROUND the bush. "Travis Van Orden is your father," she admitted. She paced with her hands in the pockets of her dress. I guessed she was more comfortable discussing things like wing spans, jet fuel, and cost figures than the deeply personal stuff we were getting into. She turned to look at me. "Travis didn't know, back then. Does he know now?"

I shook my head. "I'm sure he doesn't realize that I'm his child."

"How did you find out?"

"I put two and two together and guessed. From the minute I told her who I was, Colette Van Orden wanted me out of town. I'm sure she's the one who even wrote me an unsigned note telling me to leave. Since then, she's offered me money not to say why I came to Greendale. If I were Travis's daughter, she'd see that as a threat, I suppose. She'd be afraid I'd come between them. I had found out that you and Mr. Van Orden were high school sweethearts, and he told me himself that you'd met again one more time in Kansas City, about twenty years ago. I thought it might be more like nineteen years when I would have been conceived. If I was wrong, then there was no reason for Colette to be so against me."

"She did know about you, back then," Teal admitted. "I think I'd better tell you all about it. I was very ill that winter of 1964-65. Some kind of flu that just went on and on, besides my being pregnant. I had gone to Greendale to rest, maybe a month or two, I thought. Trav wasn't there. He was in a VA Hospital in Kansas City for a series of operations. The weather was ghastly; it snowed for weeks on end, blizzard after blizzard. I couldn't get out of town. Everything had stopped, we were snowed in."

"That's why I was born in Greendale, then? You couldn't get back to Wichita?"

"Yes." She sighed. "You were born at home, at Mother's. Mother delivered you with her own hands. Maybe that had something to do with what she did. Was behind her attachment for you." Teal looked at me for a long moment before she went on. "This is going to sound harsh, Bryn, and I hope you'll understand. I would have had an abortion, but I waited too long; I was sick and you were well on the way. So my only recourse, I felt, was to give you up for adoption after you were born."

I tried to pretend she was talking about someone else, so it wouldn't bother me too much. "It's all right," I told Teal because I wanted her to go on. I wanted to hear all of it.

"Mother and I had argued about what to do about you for weeks before you were born. If I could have gotten away from her, I would have."

"She thought you should keep me?"

"Oh, yes, definitely." Teal groaned. "You were family, she insisted; our blood was in you; no way could we give you away to strangers. She thought I was a monster to even think of giving you up. But Bryn, I *was* thinking of you, too. I wanted you to have a good, normal family life. I didn't dream I would get pregnant at that age. I didn't think I could be a good enough parent."

"So what happened then?" I asked around the lump in my throat.

"Mother knew that Travis had fathered you. I was sick with a fever a lot of the time and I talked. I was very much in love with Trav, Bryn; I always will be. Anyway, Mother decided that if I didn't want—you, then Travis should bring you up since he was your fattier. He was out of town, so Mother took it upon herself to talk to Colette Van Orden ' about it—"

"Jeez!" I exclaimed.

"Right." Teal nodded. "Colette wanted nothing to do with my child, as you might well expect. She made all kinds of threats against Mother and me if Travis were to ever find out about you. She was so afraid of losing him. I think she always knew she was second choice and that their marriage hung together by a thin thread. Maybe she thought if Trav were told he had a child, by me, he would want both of us, and he would leave her."

"I still don't know how I ended up with Gram, and not you?"

"I'm getting to that. I was still in bed, in lousy shape after your delivery. By now, Mother was fed up with all of us, with the whole damn world, except you. She really cared about you. You were only three days old when she — when she packed you up and made her way on foot through that terrible snow to where she could catch a bus, six miles away in Mumford. She just up and took off with you—!" Teal looked shocked by it, still.

The silence was heavy in the room. I sat with my arm over my face, leaning back against the pillow on Teal's couch. I could hear Teal moving quietly again, back and forth. In a while, she went on. "For the next three years, Mother was on the move with you, crossing the country, stopping here and there for a month, or longer, to work. I was so worried. I couldn't imagine how she'd manage to take care of you. The two of you were always one jump ahead of the detectives I'd hired to find you. You were about three years old when you were finally traced to a remote little logging town out in Oregon."

"Lost Creek." I thought about it for a moment. "You found me, but you didn't come after me. I would remember."

Teal shook her head. "I talked to Mother by telephone. She threatened to move again with you, and she would have before I could have gotten there. Also, three years had passed. By then, I'd been offered the position of assistant to the president of Trans-Wings. I couldn't have given you much time. I felt you were used to Mother, by then, must be reasonably happy and might not want to be uprooted, taken from her. So right or wrong, Bryn, I gave up the fight. I agreed to give Mother legal custody of you. I let her adopt you. Mother still had terrible feelings for me; she insisted that she wanted nothing from me. But I sent the checks, anyway; and when they didn't come back I believed the money was being used. I thought things were okay."

I nearly forgot that Teal was in the room, I went so deep into thought about Gram. Gram's behavior hadn't been smart, altogether; but it was plain she had felt responsible for me. She must have cared a lot to go to such drastic measures for me. That was a kind of love, had to be. Gram could have abandoned me to adoptive parents as Teal had wanted to do. Gram would have gotten by easier if she'd had only herself to look out for. But maybe she hadn't wanted to be alone; she loved me even if she couldn't show it in the usual ways. She might even have wanted to be different man she was, but didn't know how. If only I'd known this whole story when she was alive—

Teal said something, and I looked up, startled to see tears flowing down her face. She was visibly shaken. "I know how you must hate me, Bryn, with reason; but could we hug just a little? I feel so alone—"

I nodded. "I'd say it's overdue." I got up and went to her with my arms outstretched. We held one another for a long time, sobbing. Teal had had her own painful times, her own losses. I wanted to comfort her, as much as I wanted her to care for me. "I was so afraid you wouldn't want anything to do with me," I confessed, wiping my face.

She kept her arm around me as she led the way to the couch where we sat down. "God"—she reached up to touch my face—"we have so much catching up to do, Bryn. I still don't know if I'm the motherly type. I'm old enough to be a grandmother, for pity's sake. But I'm willing to try. I'll be your friend. I'll do anything for you that I can. If you want it, maybe in time we can be the way we should— mother and daughter."

I confessed through tears of wonder and joy, "I've already gotten more than I asked for, or dreamed would happen. It's enough for now. But maybe I can come to see you now and then. I'm hoping for a career; maybe as a photographer. The next few years I'll be at college, probably at KU with Rom, so that won't be far away. Is that all right with you?"

"I'd consider myself very lucky." Teal nodded. "I have to confess, I haven't been altogether pleased lately with the way my life has shaped up. I was so sure I wanted a great deal of money, like our family—the Halic generation—used to have. A career, all this—" She waved an arm at the luxurious room. "You see, I had a mortal fear of poverty. I had enough of it when I was little. But there are times when I think I've overshot my mark. I'd like to get back to simpler things. You asked once this evening if I'd ever wanted to see you. Well, there was a time when I seriously considered going out to Oregon, where you were. I had it in mind to chuck everything, buy a beach-front cottage out there, go barefoot." She laughed. "And make seashell necklaces for a living. God, Bryn, you can't know how good that still sounds."

"Maybe we can take a trip back there together some-time," I suggested. "I love the state of Oregon, even if things were rough for Gram and me there. I'd love to show you Oregon."

She took my hands in hers. "Let's do it. Next summer, okay?"

I was glad we were more or less comfortable with each other by now. And I felt it would get even better in the future. But the hour was late, and I didn't want to wear out my welcome this first time. Saying goodnight, we hugged again. "Thank you for everything," I said. "I sure didn't know what might happen, when I rang your doorbell."

She looked me over for some time before she said, "You're such a nice kid, Bryn. Honest, straightforward, strong. I like your style. I wish I could take the credit. Come see me again, child. Soon. I'm going to be thinking of myself as a mother, from now on. It ought to be easy with a kid like you. We'll see how it goes."

"We'll see," I agreed. "I've never had a mother before, so it will be strange for me, too." I felt with the main hurdle over, we both could learn.

LATER, DRIVING THE TURNPIKE TOWARD GREENDALE, I saw what an incredibly lovely night it was under that spacious, star-speckled Kansas sky. I reached out and flicked on the radio, beginning to hum. I wasn't the least displeased with my initial visit with Teal. She'd told me all that I wanted to know: my birth, about Travis.

The more I thought about him, the more I knew I had to get to know him better so that I could determine for myself how he might react to the news that he had a daughter. I didn't think he had long, not too many years left, and there was a chance I could bring him a lot of happiness. If it turned out I really believed telling him would do him good, rather than harm, then I would have to tell him. And Colette could handle it however she might.

It amazed me, I was thinking, too, what the mind could imagine when it didn't have the facts. I didn't have to wonder and worry any more that there was murder and mayhem in my past. Gram must have thought, though, that it was bad enough that I was better off not to hear. But really, it was only people being people, making mistakes and covering up with further mistakes. Often not realizing the needless unhappiness and worry they caused. I supposed something similar to my story happened to somebody, somewhere, most every day.

No great tragedy, my past. At that moment, I saw the

whole of it more like a prism of shadow, light, and colors. The shadows represented the unhappier things, and the light was the good. The colors were love. Purple was the color of the deep love Gram—Ivana—had with Gamble Jones, my grandfather. The sad love of my birth parents, Teal and Travis, was blue. Orange was a good color for the warm feelings I shared with my new-found cousins, the Fontaines. And yes, Gram loved me. Her color was a small red flame that flickered on when her capacity for most other feelings was gone.

My love for Rom? Our color was fresh new green, with a lush growing season ahead. How far was it to Arlington, I wondered. Tomorrow was Saturday, a free day for me. If I went back to Greendale and got a little sleep, could I be there by breakfast time?

A look at: Willow Whip

*From award-winning author Irene Bennett Brown comes a heartwarming story of a young girl determined to make it possible for her constantly moving farmer family to buy a farm that she has come to love and wants to live on permanentl*y.

Could the Faber family really afford a farm of their own? Could they stop moving from place to place? Her father has almost given up hope, but for Willow Faber, the only dream worth having is a farm of their own.

The Fabers are tenant farmers. They move almost every year trying to find a better place. But no farm will ever compare to the one Willow calls "The Ranch." Once a Pony Express stop, it is old, but solid and pleasant, and Willow is willing to do everything she can to make it theirs.

For a long year Willow does little but plan and work and save, pushing herself—and her family—to the brink, earning herself the nickname "Willow The Whip." She sacrifices everything, including all of the things she had hoped to gain by staying in one place. Only near disaster helps her understand what she has lost and all that she still has to gain.

AVAILABLE NOW

About the Author

Irene Bennett Brown is an award-winning author who enjoys using Kansas—where she was born—as background for her historical novels. Previous to her ten novels for adults, Brown authored nine young adult novels. *Before the Lark* won a Western Writers of America Spur Award, was nominated for the Mark Twain Award, and received other honors. Her other YA novels include *To Rainbow Valley, Run from a Scarecrow, Skitterbrain, Willow Whip, Morning Glory Afternoon, Answer Me Answer Me, I Loved You Logan McGee,* and *Just Another Gorgeous Guy.*

Her most recent Nickel Hill series include *Miss Royal's Mules, Tangled Times, Somebody's Business* and *One True Deed.* All are adult sequels to *Before the Lark.*

She lives with her husband, Bob—a retired research chemist—on two fruitful acres along the Santiam River in Oregon.

Visit her website at <u>irenebennettbrown.net</u> for more information.